The Rock Star Wants A Wife

DEMELZA CARLTON

Book 5 in the Romance Island Resort series

DEDICATION

This book is for all the wonderful people in and around
Broome who went above and beyond to show a
tourist/researcher all the beauties of the Kimberley, from
sleeping in a tent and swag right up to staying in a five star
resort.
Even those who didn't believe I was writing a book, let
alone six.

ONE

Cruise ships were to hangovers what hell was to a burns victim: torture. Penny grabbed the toilet seat and hauled herself up off the bathroom floor. No matter how nauseous she felt, she had nothing left to barf up. She remembered that much from last night. She couldn't have drunk enough of that cheap tequila, then. Or maybe that scummy Mexican restaurant had watered it down. That's what it was. They'd poisoned her instead of getting her drunk, so that's why she felt so sick. She remembered every heaving, hoiking moment with gut-wrenching clarity, so she couldn't have been drugged.

Getting laid would be infinitely preferable to lying on the tiny bathroom floor, sandwiched between the shower and the toilet, wondering if she'd vomit her guts up before drifting into a doze.

Someone hammered on her cabin door. "Penny, time to go. You've got breakfast shift, remember?"

Breakfast. Good thing she only had to cook it, not eat it.

Five minutes later, showered and changed into an apprentice chef's uniform that felt fresher than she did, Penny staggered out of her cramped cabin, along the passage that led to the cruise ship's kitchens.

"Late again," growled Pierre, the head chef. Actually, his name was Peter, she'd found out one night in Sydney, when some drunken blokes had hailed him as *Poiter*, a fellow Collingwood fan, who had to help them celebrate the football team's victory. Sadly, knowing his real name hadn't made him any nicer to her. If anything, he just hated her more for it. "I told you, you turn up on time and do your job, or I'll find another apprentice who will."

Penny nodded and tied on her apron, keeping her head down so she didn't inhale the heady scents of food that she didn't want.

"You're on pancakes this morning," he added maliciously, his eyes daring her to protest.

Pancakes were usually a kitchenhand's job, not a trained chef like she was, but Penny didn't mind the mindless task of spooning, watching, flipping and sliding the perfect circles of fluffiness onto people's plates. She'd first learned to make them on a Macca's grill, and she'd only improved her skills since. Penny was proud of her pancakes.

She fell into an easy rhythm, pouring, flipping and sliding, until she found herself smiling. Squeals of delight sounded from child passengers as they first saw their personal stack of pancakes. Oh, but there was always one...

"I want ones like we had at Disneyland. I want...Mickey Mouse!" screeched today's brat of indeterminate sex, screwing up its face.

Penny didn't miss a beat. Two ears, a round face, then

another, and another…within a few minutes she had a perfect stack of mouse-head pancakes fit for the royal little shit.

"Ooh, look, Minnie Mouse," a little girl breathed, her eyes shining. "Please, Mummy, can I have those, too?"

Penny liked this mother. Mummy pursed her lips, duck-fashion, clearly having no trouble refusing her child's whim.

Of course it was the overindulged little shits who always got what they wanted, while more deserving people, like Penny and this polite little girl, didn't get a stinking thing.

"I can do it. It's no trouble," Penny found herself saying. Well, it was true. It's not like she had a queue at the pancake station. The dining room was nearly empty this early in the morning.

One of the kitchenhands brought out another jug of batter, spiriting away the empties. Penny inhaled deeply as she tested the batter. It had to have the right texture, flowing across the grill, with just the right amount of froth.

Mmm, vanilla and eggs, with the salty undertaste of the real butter she greased the grill with. Maybe she was hungry after all. She'd have to wait a long time before she could sneak a plate of pancakes out for a breakfast break, though. Pierre's eagle eyes saw everything.

Sighing, Penny told her rumbling stomach to shut the fuck up as she counted the minutes until the end of Pierre's shift and her self-imposed starvation.

TWO

The familiar, heart-shaped island came into view, and Xan felt an unexpected surge of happiness at the sight. It was her island home now, she reasoned, though not entirely the paradise it appeared. She still had to share it with the man who stood on the rise overlooking the helipad, his arms folded.

The helicopter landed with a soft bump. "Thanks, Shou," Xan told the pilot, patting his shoulder as she slid out the door. Instinctively, she ducked her head until she was clear of the still-spinning blades, so she didn't see the other woman coming the other way until she almost bumped into her.

"Watch where you're going!" Gaia snarled, sidestepping. She swept past Xan, holding her head high despite the whirling death overhead.

Idly, Xan wondered what would happen to the woman's

vast fortune if the billionaire lost her life in an unfortunate accident with a helicopter rotor. Then she remembered the magazines she'd seen at the airport. The billionaire was engaged to Jay, apparently. So the rock star would probably inherit everything. As if he didn't already have enough money. Admittedly, it would be a small price to pay, knowing a rich man had grown immeasurably richer, if it meant the world was rid of the unpleasant Gaia Vasse.

The helicopter door slammed, jolting Xan out of her thoughts, so she noticed with chagrin that Gaia was safe in the plexiglass bubble, soon to be spirited away from her island. Xan's island, not Gaia's. Well, Jay's island, really, but she managed Romance Island Resort, so that made the whole island her responsibility.

"You don't know how good it is to see you."

Xan found herself enveloped in an unexpected hug from none other than Jay Felix. He seemed to realise his mistake before she opened her mouth to demand he let her go.

"Sorry, Xan. It's been tough here without you."

She acknowledged his apology – the first she'd ever heard him utter. "I bet. I'm gone for less than a fortnight and you get engaged. Again."

His expression darkened. "I'm what? To who?"

Xan's eyes followed the helicopter's flight. "Your billionaire, of course. You're in all the gossip magazines. I think I might have some copies in my carry-on." Xan wet her lips. "Before I left, you were absolutely in love with that travel agent, I thought. But that billionaire snapped her fingers and you sold the ordinary girl to the press." Her heart hardened against the thoughtless rock star. He'd unleashed a media storm on the poor girl, until she'd fled from her country town home to who knew where. Hopefully not the media or fickle Mr Felix, anyway.

"I'd rather kill myself than spend another minute in that crazy bitch's company. We're not engaged, and I hope I never see her again." Jay narrowed his eyes as he watched the helicopter disappear. "Do you know what she did to Flavia?"

It couldn't have been worse than his media frenzy, Xan thought but didn't say.

"She got one of her staff to hack her email, then leaked everything to the press. Even I didn't know where Flavia lived, but Gaia had reporters on her doorstep, harassing her at work." Jay looked pained. "I'm used to the media, but Flavia...she couldn't take it. She disappeared. Wouldn't take my calls."

Xan let this sink in. "You mean you didn't set the media on her?"

Jay snorted. "Since when do I ever let reporters near anyone? Not even the girls in the band. I'm the media hog for a fucking reason, you know."

"And here I thought you were just an attention whore," Xan said.

A normal man would have been insulted. Not Jay. His frown broke into what Xan thought was a rueful smile. "Well, yeah, there's that. But someone had to take all the media's attention. The girls didn't want to do it, so that left me. Lucky me, the press fucking loved me. Especially if I got my kit off. Just the shirt was enough, Jo said, but there was this one time I wanted to go skinnydipping in Sydney Harbour, after a show at the Opera House, so me and a bunch of groupies – "

Xan covered her ears. "I don't want to know." She lowered her hands, then added, "Nice catching up and all, but I have work to do. I managed to score quite the coup for the resort." She allowed herself a satisfied smile. "On top of the deal with Vasse Prospecting and *Due South*, we're now the official venue for the final season of *Farmer Bags A Bride*, the reality TV dating show." If she sounded a little smug, it didn't matter. She was allowed, damn it.

"Farmer bags a bride? What, like in a sack? Kidnapping women? How the fuck is that entertainment?" Jay asked.

Xan wasn't sure if he was joking or serious. "It doesn't matter. What does is that the farmers and the film crew will be here soon to do some of the preliminary shooting. It's free publicity for the resort, and we get paid a hefty fee for all the accommodation and facility hire. Jo nearly kissed me when she found out." Fortunately, Jay didn't look like he shared his sister's enthusiasm for the deal, so Xan shouldered her bag and headed home to her house overlooking the lagoon.

Ah, paradise. Yes, she was home.

THREE

Never…eating…pancakes…EVER…again, Penny swore, grabbing a wad of paper towel to wipe her face. She rinsed her mouth, then ran the water a little longer, letting it flush away the evidence that she'd thrown up in the sink. This wasn't a normal tequila-induced hangover. She knew that now. Someone must have tried to poison her, either while she was on shore leave or when she got back.

Tess, her roommate. Tess had been angry at her since she caught Tess bonking on her bunk with two of the fitness instructors. As if the girl had any right to be angry when it was Penny's bed she'd been screwing two guys on. Guys who hadn't apologised or even stopped. No, they'd asked her if she wanted to join in.

Double stuffed by the buff personal trainers? It sounded like one of the porn films in the pay-per-view library the guests got access to. Or one of the erotica books in the library at the resort where she used to work. Penny had refused, then climbed up to Tess's bunk and tried to fall asleep over the grunting and moaning going on down below.

Tess had threatened to reveal Penny's smoking habit to the staff supervisor if Penny spoke a word about what she'd seen that night. Crew weren't allowed to smoke aboard the cruise ship, though guests could; lighting a single cigarette could lose Penny her job. But some nights when Tess was too loud with her boyfriends, Penny would dress in civilian clothes, hike up to the highest deck and breathe in as much tarry goodness as she could suck into her lungs. No one recognised her in the dark, or so she'd thought. God, she wanted one now, to burn the taste of bile out of the back of her throat.

"You're fired."

Penny lifted her impossibly heavy head to peer blearily at Pierre. *Poiter*. "What for?"

Pierre sniffed. "For showing up to work with a hangover again. I told you, I don't tolerate staff who drink to excess before a shift. You are here to cook magnificent meals, not be sick in the sink."

"I didn't drink a lot last night. I'm sick," Penny insisted, as fear clutched at her heart. She couldn't lose this job. No one else would take her if Pierre fired her. She'd never be a proper chef.

"Your roommate says you were so sick last night, she had to go to the next room to use the bathroom. Don't lie to me. You are a disgrace!" Pierre roared.

Maybe she did have a hangover. Her head sure hurt when he shouted like that. "I'm sick," she mumbled.

"When the ship docks in port, you will leave it. Until then, report to the housekeeping manager. If you're not working on the ship, you'll have to pay for your passage." Pierre's malevolent smile made her teeth hurt.

Pay? Penny didn't have the money to pay for luxury cruise ship accommodation. Why else had she been drinking tequila last night? If she'd been able to afford better, she'd have been drinking it. "No. Just…let me work until we reach port. I won't drink any more. I promise." She wouldn't keep a drink down, anyway.

"You're not working in my kitchen!"

He was a god-damn drama queen. "Fine. How about here, then? I'll wash dishes?" She pointed at the benchtop dishwasher and the sinks big enough to stand in. She'd worked plenty such shifts when she was in high school. Anything was better than paying for things she couldn't afford.

He eyed her for an interminable moment. "Very well, then. But if I find a single plate that is not perfectly clean…" He shook his fist.

Penny nodded, not really caring. As soon as he was out of sight, she slithered down the wall to sit on the floor. How was she supposed to wash dishes when she was too weak to stand?

Didn't matter, she told herself, grabbing the edge of the sink to hoist herself up again. She'd lean on that for the whole shift if she had to. At least she had plenty of places to be sick if she needed. Drains galore.

A grim smile graced her lips as the first cart of dirty dishes arrived.

She got to work, loading the plates into the dishwasher,

then unloading them onto the drying cart, where they'd stay for barely long enough to drip dry before the kitchenhands came to collect them for the next wave of breakfast customers. With every clink of a plate settling in its rack, Penny's fury built.

When she found out who'd poisoned her, she'd make her pay, Penny swore.

FOUR

"Of course they're still bachelors. Gay marriage isn't legal yet in Australia, is it?" Jay drawled.

Xan hushed him, hoping they hadn't heard him over the thumping rotor blades, and stepped forward to welcome the farmer bachelors to the resort. They both seemed far too impressed with the island to even look at her, but Xan had grown used to that. Most of the day trippers looked the same when they first walked up the jetty. Hell, she'd probably been just as wide-eyed on her first day here. Less than a year ago, but it felt like longer. Much longer.

Both bachelors looked like they'd stepped right off a working farm into the helicopter. Both wore dusty boots, shorts and shirts, like locals.

"Where are you from?" she asked.

"Kununurra," said one.

"Derby," said the other.

"Which town did you fly from, then?" Xan asked.

One grinned. "Town? Nah, I didn't waste time driving into town. All the pilots round here know my station. I bet there isn't a single one who hasn't helped with mustering one time or another."

The other bloke cleared his throat. "I only bought the station a year ago. Sold my house in Hedland and cashed in my redundancy payment to get the place. I've had a manager running the place for me, but I'm learning to do it meself. Especially if I have a wife to help." He puffed out his chest.

Mm, slave labour, Xan thought, flashing a bland smile. She shouldn't judge. There might be women absolutely champing at the bit to spend the rest of their lives with bachelors just like these two. Not everyone wanted to stay single because the alternative – men – was too much trouble. She'd vicariously enjoy the perfect love lives of the resort library full of fictional heroines, and never need to bother with the real, imperfect thing, ever again.

Paige, the reality show's host, appeared then, accompanied by two cameramen. She waved madly for Xan and Jay to move out of the shot, and Xan was only too happy to oblige. Jay was slower to move, but he did get out of the way eventually. In fact, when Xan turned to see where he'd disappeared to, he was already slouching off down the path to the lagoon.

After a moment, she decided that she wasn't needed, either, so Xan headed for her office, resolving to check on the film crew's progress later in the day.

FIVE

Three days later, when the ship pulled into Broome, it was quarantined, to Penny's satisfaction. She hadn't been poisoned, after all. The ship had suffered a norovirus outbreak, the ship's medical officer said. Penny recovered within a day or two, but Pierre and Tess were two of the first to come down with it, followed by pretty much every passenger who'd eaten breakfast that day. Off the plates Pierre had forced her to wash.

There'd been talk of ending the cruise early, so the cruise company could disinfect the ship. That would teach them to employ arseholes like Pierre. It wasn't until Penny disembarked amid a pack of pale-faced passengers that she realised she had a problem. The cruise company had paid for all of them to be put up in the hotels in town, which left precious little accommodation for her. The crew remained aboard, forced to clean the ship from top to bottom. Penny didn't envy them.

She'd tried reasoning with Pierre, when it became apparent that she truly had been sick, but he held stubbornly to his decision. She no longer worked for him, and the only reference she'd get from him would be a bad one.

So she shouldered her bag and boarded one of the courtesy buses provided to transport the passengers into town. She wasn't sure what to do next, but she had enough money to buy a beer, and God knew she needed a drink in this heat.

There was standing room only in the Roey – not something she'd often seen in the town's iconic pub. Nevertheless, she sidled through the crowd to reach the bar, where she waited for ages before the bartender so much as acknowledged her.

"What'll it be?" the woman asked.

Penny waved her hand. "Whatever pint's cheapest." Today she didn't care what sort of beer she got, as long as it was ice cold. Sure enough, it was.

She counted out the last coins in her purse to pay for it, feeling her face grow red with shame.

"I take it you're not one of the cruise passengers?" the bartender asked.

Penny shook her head.

"Backpacker? Looking for work?"

Penny set her beer down on the bar. What did she have to lose? It's not like she had a job any more. "Yeah."

"We could do with an extra waitress today. Have you ever waited tables before? Served in a bar?"

Penny sighed. "Yeah, and worked in the kitchen, too.

I'm an apprentice chef, but I thought I'd take a break for a bit."

The bartender extended a hand across the bar. "Freena. I'll pay you fifteen bucks an hour for as long as I need you today, and at the end, we'll talk about tomorrow, maybe."

Fifteen was better than nothing. "Sure. I'm Penny."

Freena nodded. "Grab an apron in the kitchen. Tell Dirk you're the new waitress. He'll give you a rundown on where to put your orders and where to collect them." She eyed Penny's bag. "You can put your things in the office in the back."

Penny emptied her beer and wiped her mouth with the back of her hand. Take that, Pierre, she thought. Not off the ship for an hour and already she had a new job.

SIX

"There. Done." Xan switched off her computer, stood and stretched. She'd caught glimpses of the film crew and the two bachelors through her window over the course of the afternoon, but she'd been good and stayed at her desk, doing her job. Now, it was knock-off time. It would be the most natural thing in the world to stroll past while they were filming, and casually ask about their progress.

She picked up her phone and dialled the extension for IT. Before Seb could finish his greeting, she cut him off. "Where are they?"

"Clustered around North Beach, near the treeline," he replied promptly.

Xan smothered a laugh. Trust the nosy IT boys to know their every movement. The show's bubbly hostess seemed to have a talent for making men melt. Except for Jay, oddly. There must be a history there, she decided. "Thanks," she said to Seb, then ended the call.

She enjoyed the short walk to the beach, shucking off her shoes so she could feel the sand between her toes. She wasn't surprised to find the farmers and their film crew precisely where Seb had said, but she was surprised to see Jay there. Paige divided her attention between the farmers and Jay, though Jay didn't seem to notice her admiring glances. The farmers appeared too awed by Jay to do more than stammer out responses to Paige's questions, which made the woman snap in irritation.

Filming was not going well, Xan decided.

"I'm looking for a girl who can cook and clean and isn't afraid of cows. She doesn't have to be a beauty queen, but she should be fit, you know, like me." The farmer flexed his biceps.

The other farmer nodded thoughtfully, looking like he approved.

Xan choked back laughter.

Paige looked like she was going to explode.

"Nah, mate, no girl will go for that. You gotta romance it up a bit," Jay said.

They all stared.

"Say how pretty your farm is, or how awesome it is to have…however many head of cattle you have. But how it gets lonely, so you work out a lot and get pretty active, so you'd love to have someone to share it with. Love and laughter over a delicious meal at the end of a hard day's work. Help picking the names of this year's new calves. You're looking for a partner, a soulmate, to share stuff with. Some mushy shit like that." Jay shrugged.

More nods of approval, from both blokes this time.

"How would you do it, then?" ventured the one who hadn't spoken yet. "If you wanted a wife."

Xan expected Jay to laugh off the suggestion, but he surprised her, again. Maybe it was how intently Paige stared at him as she signalled for the cameraman to start filming.

"Mr Felix, what are you looking for in a wife?" Paige asked.

"I've met a lot of ladies, lovely ladies, in my career. All of them beautiful and talented in their own way. But you know what? I never met the One."

"What's so special about the One?" Paige prompted.

"The One…she'd capture my heart. Every touch or smile would strike me like a bolt of lightning. We'd share everything and we'd be equal in everything. For every time I save her, she'll save me right back. She'd be the melody to my bass line. She'll inspire love songs so beautiful I could seduce the whole world, but there's only one woman in the world I want. The one woman who will help me write my first true love song – one to last a lifetime."

Even Xan found herself sighing at Jay's words. The farmers still looked awed, but now they also looked…inspired.

One of them traded places with Jay. He cleared his throat. "When I stand on the highest point on my farm, all the land I can see is mine, because I have one of the biggest cattle stations in the country. You'd think with all that, I'd be satisfied, but it's a lonely life. No one to share it with when the sun sinks into the desert, or when the dawn lights up the eastern ranges just right…"

Now it was Jay's turn to nod, but Paige's smile said she approved, too.

The rest of the filming went quite quickly after that, with Paige declaring a wrap just over an hour later. The blokes seemed to have bonded over the experience, and were now offering to shout each other and Jay beers in the pub afterwards.

After hearing spiels about how miserably lonely it was in the Kimberley for a single bloke, Xan decided she'd like to alleviate a little loneliness of her own, and offered to join Paige for a drink in the Jungle, too. So they took a table in one corner while the blokes claimed one by the bar, and Xan sipped her way through a ginger beer as she and Paige made small talk about the show.

Paige couldn't say much, of course, but she was happy to explain some of the basics. The interviews they'd done today would be edited down to under five minutes, before they were uploaded to the network's website. Then they'd open the call for potential brides. In the past, they'd sometimes gotten thousands of applications, and the studio staff would narrow it down to the ladies who ticked all the boxes on the bachelors' sometimes extensive lists. One bloke had only liked redheads. One particularly short bloke had insisted anyone taller than his shoulder need not apply. One of them had owned an oyster farm, so the girls all had to like seafood and not be allergic.

Once they had a shortlist for each of the bachelors, they gave the lists to the men. Each bloke got his own list, and he had to narrow it down to twenty women he'd like to meet, though only eight would make it onto the show. Officially, that was because sometimes the girls couldn't get the time off work, or they had other commitments that meant they couldn't make the filming dates, or the farmstay.

"Farmstay?" Xan asked.

The bachelors interviewed all eight girls and got to pick four favourites, Paige explained, who would be invited to stay on the bloke's farm for a couple of weeks. A film crew would go out to each farm with the girls, to record pretty much everything. Every kiss, every alone moment, which the crew sometimes had to arrange, planning dates for the couple either on the farm or at a nearby town. The bachelor would send two of the girls home within the first week, but the remaining two would stay for the duration, and meet up with some of his family and friends, before he had to make his final decision.

"And they're expected to get married? Just like that?" Xan said, trying to hide her incredulity.

Paige laughed. "It's encouraged, and the studio offers them a pretty sweet bonus if they propose on the show, and then invite the host and camera crew to the wedding, so we can broadcast it between seasons, but it doesn't happen very often. The weddings do get a lot of viewers, though, and you see it in the boost in the next season's numbers. We actually have a pretty high success rate – a lot of the couples stay together long after the show. Some of them do get married, and some even have kids."

Xan glanced at the two farmers. "Do you think they will…?

Paige donned her professional smile, the same sort Xan wore when she was being deliberately vague. "You never know for sure until you see them with the girls. It's all about chemistry."

Jay slapped his hands on their table, startling Xan. "It sure is, but I already told you, they won't. They have all the chemistry they need right at that table. Fresh beers, too. I figured I didn't want to feel like the third wheel over there, so I said my goodnights, and now I'll say the same to you ladies. It is time for me to watch…the *Simpsons*." He strode out of the pub.

"I'm sure that's some sort of euphemism for adult films," Xan said, watching him go.

"I doubt it," Paige replied. "If he wanted to watch *Martian Buttsex 69*, Jay would probably say so, just to see our expressions. And, like me, he is a big fan of the *Simpsons*." She rose and excused herself, pleading an early start the next day.

Xan headed home soon after, intrigued by Paige's easy explanation about TV matchmaking and trying not to wonder why there was more than one film about…what was it? Martian butt sex? Urgh. No, she would NOT search the internet to find out more about it. It'd be faster to ask the IT guys, anyway. And she wouldn't have to see pictures.

SEVEN

Pierre was right, Penny reflected glumly, untying her apron. She wouldn't get work as an apprentice chef again in a hurry. Oh, sure, she had a waitressing job, and she'd even found a place to live in a sharehouse in town without too much trouble, but she was as far from becoming a qualified chef as the day she jumped aboard that cruise ship. The universe hated her, that was why.

As she cleaned up the last of the tables, she picked up a copy of the day's *West*. On the cover was a woman in chef's whites, holding up some sort of trophy she'd won in a competition. Glancing around to make sure no one needed her, Penny took a moment to read the article.

Penny's surprise increased with each word she read. Far from being a trained chef, the woman was a mother and office worker in one of the regional towns down the coast. Yet the meals she'd cooked as part of some reality TV program had earned her the status of one of Australia's celebrity chefs.

The newspaper dropped from her hand. If she went on one of those programs, she wouldn't need to finish her apprenticeship. Her reputation would speak for itself, and Pierre could go screw himself. She'd be able to open her own restaurant, and never have to look to some overbearing man for direction again. She'd be in charge.

EIGHT

Paige staggered into Xan's office and slumped into her client chair without saying a word. Her stricken expression said plenty, though.

Xan set down her pen. The quotes for the new glass-bottomed boat for the lagoon could wait. "Who died?" she asked lightly.

Paige glared.

Xan felt a chill of dread that she'd have a corpse to deal with.

"I've lost two farmers," Paige bit out through gritted teeth.

Xan reached for her phone. "I'll call IT. They can find anyone on the island in less than a minute."

Paige laughed harshly. "Oh, I know where they are. In one of your hotel rooms, locked in behind a DO NOT DISTURB sign."

"I can override any door lock in the resort, if necessary," Xan offered.

"After all you said about guest privacy, and how important it is to the resort, you'd force open a guest's door?" Paige mocked.

Xan shook her head, wishing the other woman would stop talking in riddles. "Okay, none of this makes any sense. Please tell me what's happened, what course of action you'd like to take, and how my staff and I can help." She thought her voice did a pretty good job at hiding her irritation.

Paige gave a mirthless smile. "Well, it looks like after yesterday's filming, our two farmers got to drinking in your pub. Once the beer had been flowing freely for a few hours, they became the best of mates. Good enough mates to share a few secrets. Turns out they were hiding the same secret, and when one of them spilled the beans…"

"Congratulations!" Jay burst into Xan's office, beaming. "I bet you never expected your matchmaking to pay off so quickly. C'mon, that has to be a record for the show."

Xan rubbed her temples. If anything, Jay made even less sense than Paige.

"Where are they now?" Paige demanded.

Jay pulled up a chair for himself. "They saw me taking my morning swim in the lagoon, and decided they wanted one, too. I told them about my favourite hidden beach, and I bet they're getting all romantic right there now."

"With who?" Xan asked. "You haven't even asked their prospective brides to apply yet. You can't tell me both of those blokes have suddenly turned into Don Juans overnight and both seduced women they've just met? The only women in the pub last night were us!"

Jay just shook his head, while Paige's expression grew more thunderous.

"Ah, c'mon, Paige. Don't be so pissed off. I told you yesterday they were gay. You didn't believe me then, but you can't deny it now. They're out of the closet and thrilled to have found a kindred spirit. It'd be an awesome line to take with the show. Call it *Farmer Bags A Partner* instead and turn it into the first gay dating show in Australia. You could always throw in the occasional straight guy, too, just to mix things up a bit. I'm sure you'll have plenty of takers. I mean, yesterday, for a minute there, even I considered – "

"I called the studio this morning," Paige interrupted. "They said they won't champion gay marriage in Australia in the current climate. Their ratings would plummet. And if I can't find two replacement farmers who like women, they'll cancel the show entirely."

It was Xan's turn to drop into despair. "What? No! I've cancelled dozens of day trips to fit with your filming schedule. All the tourism operators in town are sponsoring this thing. You can't cancel the show!"

"We had trouble enough finding these two blokes. No one wants to go on a reality dating show any more. The drama we put the blokes through on camera, the pressure they're under to find love and make a decision in that short time…these are guys who struggle to ask a girl out on a date, they're so shy and awkward. With budget cuts, we can't afford another country-wide call for bachelors. My budget's effectively zero for the search."

"What if you were willing to negotiate a bit with the blokes? Dial down the drama a bit and let them see some of the raw footage before it goes to air, so they have a better idea of what the girls are like, and what your viewers will see?" Jay suggested.

"Not a hope in hell. The network executives will never buy it. No one has that kind of pull with them." Paige shook her head violently.

"Bet I could swing it," Jay said.

"You'd still need to find farmers – " Paige began.

"Nah, I was thinking me."

Xan and Paige stared at him.

Paige recovered first. "You want to pretend to be a farmer and make me find you a suitable wife? Even for you, that's crazy. We'd be overwhelmed with applications. Half the female population – not just the ones under thirty – would apply. We'd probably get thousands of international applications, too. It'd take months just to narrow it down. And everyone knows you'll never settle down. You're the ultimate tomcat, which is why girls love you so much."

"So don't tell them who I am. Say I'm a mystery man, some sort of celebrity, but don't say who. Hide my identity from the girls until they arrive here for the meet and greet. Sure, you'll get fewer applicants, but I bet you still get quite a selection. And ones who aren't pulled in by my name, either, so maybe, if I'm really lucky, you might find me a bride."

Xan watched Jay, waiting for him to admit he was joking. He had to be. No one in their right mind would…

"Okay," Paige said. "But I don't think we could run the show with just one bachelor. Even running with two was going to be hard, because we normally have at least six. How on earth will we manage to record enough footage to fill a show about just you?"

Jay grinned. "Oh, but it's not just me. It's all about the girls, because most of your viewers are women. So have more girls. Double the number. I don't know. We got plenty of space here, and you'd originally planned to have two blokes with all their brides-to-be."

Paige tapped her chin. "But what about the farmstay? The girls are supposed to come and stay with you on your farm. We get really good ratings for the first farm episode. Viewers love watching city girls adjust to rural life."

Jay shrugged. "Does it have to be my farm?"

"Well, no, but it's not as realistic if it's not yours. I mean, the girls are supposed to be seeing if they can fit into your lifestyle, isolated out here, and this luxury resort isn't exactly slumming it."

Jay laughed. "My lifestyle, as you call it, isn't as glamorous as you think. But I meant the pearl farm, on the mainland. Yeah, they have luxury accommodation, but they also have a bush camp they run with one of the tour companies in town. It's pretty basic, but it's a step up from the old pearl divers' camp that used to be there."

Paige stared at him incredulously. "You, the rock star, would go camping?"

"Sure. I've been meaning to check it out. If I record a new album next year, I was thinking of setting some of the music videos out there."

Now it was Xan's turn to stare. "You mean you're coming out of retirement?"

Jay shrugged. "It's been a year. I don't think I'm old enough to retire. And I still got a bit of music in me. I just need to talk the girls into getting the band back together, or find someone to replace them, if they won't. I figured I'd wait until after Angel's wedding, and hit them up then. I was talking to my agent this week, and some of the offers she's had since this whole press storm with that mining billionaire are…pretty fucking awesome. I figure a season of reality TV might up the offers enough to buy me another island."

He wasn't joking, Xan realised. It made no sense, but that was Jay all over.

"So I'll run it by the studio, and if they accept, I'll speak to the sponsors, to see if they're willing to offer a bit more for the dates and such. I mean, we kept everything pretty low-key for the farmers, but a rock star would get the VIP treatment, all the way," Paige said eagerly. "We might have to change the name a bit, though, seeing as you're not really a farmer."

"Got that right. I wouldn't know what to do with a sheep, let alone a whole flock. How about *Rock Star Wants A Wife?*

Paige nodded. "I'll get right onto it. We could even use that video you recorded yesterday…"

Jay laughed. "So you did record it! I wondered." He leaned forward. "I'll have some conditions, though. Seeing as I'm saving your show and all."

Paige bit her lip, waving at him to keep talking.

"You're not putting me through the same shit you do to the normal blokes. I want access to all the footage, including your private interviews with the girls. I want to see everything before it goes to air, even if it isn't going to air."

Paige shook her head. "The studio will never go for that. If you know what's going on, there won't be any drama.

And with more girls, and only one of you, we'll need way more filler to make the show. Instead of just two weeks, we'll have to stretch it out to four. You won't have time to watch everything. And we'll be sending it back to the studio for editing, not doing it here. I can't – "

"Sure you can. Set up a temporary studio here. I'm sure the IT guys would love to hook you up with whatever equipment you need. I'll use it for music videos later, so it's no big deal to me. But I won't do it if I can't see the video. You can air whatever you like, as long as it meets with Xan's privacy guidelines for the resort…oh, wait. If we do most of the filming at Shenton Camp, we won't have to worry about that, will we? Right. I'll have access to all the video you take during the four weeks, so I can make my decision with as much background on the girls as I need."

"But the show needs drama," Paige insisted. "You won't – "

"What if I promise to propose in the final episode?" Jay demanded.

Paige seemed lost for words.

"All the drama you want. You can set up the girls' stories any way you like for the show. I'm not asking to be able to veto shit, or even try to censor it. I'm only asking to see the raw stuff, so I can make a decision on who I ask to marry me." From the triumph in Jay's eyes, he knew he had her.

"I'll have to ask the studio…" Paige said, looking doubtful.

Jay jumped to his feet. "When they agree, give Xan the schedule. This'll be fun!"

NINE

Paige left the office, muttering to herself, leaving Xan alone with Jay.

"Why?" Xan blurted out.

"Why what?" There was an edge to Jay's tone. A hostile one that told her not to pry.

Xan ignored it. "Why do you want a wife? From a reality TV show, of all things!"

Jay shrugged. "Nothing else has worked. Figured I'd try my luck. You never know." He jammed his lips shut.

"But a wife? Since I met you, you've been trying every trope in the book…no, the whole damn library, to find yourself a wife. What I don't understand is why."

Another shrug. "Angel, one of the girls in the band, is getting married. If she's doing it, then I figure it's time. The media seem to think so, too, after the way they jumped on the story Gaia fed them."

"And the reality TV angle?" Xan pressed.

"I'm used to being in the limelight. This should put paid to the rumours about me and Gaia. Figure this'll test the waters, too, see if the public's ready for me to make a comeback tour. Maybe see if they're ready to make me the rightful king of rock again." Jay's rueful grin didn't look particularly optimistic.

The strangest thought came into her head, and Xan burst out laughing. "You're on a quest!" she gasped out. "A quest to regain your throne, but first you're looking for the golden fleece!"

"I'm what?"

"Jason! Your given name is Jason, right? It's Jason and the Argonauts, with one hell of a modern spin. He climbed aboard the *Argo* with all his hero mates and headed off in search of the golden fleece to win back his throne." Xan snorted. "Bet you pick a blonde."

"I haven't read that one," Jay said. "Heard of it, yeah, but that's all. Did he get the throne, the fleece, and maybe a girl?"

Xan sobered. "Yes, but there were a few women along the way. More than one. Jason was a cheating bastard, but his wife was a witch, so she had her revenge."

Jay shivered. "Maybe it's a good thing I'm not him, then."

Now Xan had him talking, she figured she'd attempt to learn some more about her employer. "What's the deal with you and Paige?"

"We were together for a while, before Chaya made it big," Jay said curtly.

"Then you dumped her?" Xan guessed, disgust rising up

the back of her throat.

"No." Jay's gaze dropped to his clenched fists. "She was the news anchor on my first interview, the one that went viral and started it all. The band's career launched that night, and afterwards, Paige and I…well, I wasn't a rock star then. We dated for a while, like normal people, but her social media just blew up. Death threats, hate mail…there was a whole group of arseholes who sent her hourly messages about how she should kill herself. Detailed messages. Pictures and descriptions and…fuck, it's no wonder she considered it." He glanced around. "You got anything to drink?"

Xan held out her half-drunk bottle of water.

Jay waved it away. "Nah, something stronger. I need a real drink."

"I have some rum at my house," Xan began reluctantly. She pressed her lips together before she invited him home. The last place she wanted Jay to get drunk was her tiny unit.

"Me, too. Meet you on the Penguin Jetty? I'll bring the bottle." Jay strode out the door without waiting for her response.

"And glasses!" Xan shouted after him.

Jay waved to acknowledge that he'd heard, but he didn't slow.

TEN

Xan reached the jetty first. The tide was on its way in, licking hungrily at the jetty pylons. Xan's belly rumbled a response – she should have stopped to grab a bite to eat. The last thing she needed was to drink half a bottle of rum on an empty stomach.

"You hungry?"

Jay stood at the head of the jetty, with a room service tray in his arms. Xan could have hugged him. If he weren't her employer and the bane of her existence, of course.

"Yes," she admitted.

"Good. I got some fishy bite things from Catering. It said panko crumbs, prawns, squid, scallops and stuff on the menu." Jay peered under the cover. "You do eat seafood, right? I can call them and get you something else."

"I'm fine with seafood," Xan replied, catching a whiff of what Jay held. If it was the seafood tasting platter from the room service menu, there'd be fresh lobster in there somewhere. She could count on the fingers of one hand the number of times she'd eaten lobster. She'd even forgive Jay for forgetting the glasses.

He set the tray on the jetty and Xan realised she'd underestimated him, yet again. Dangling from his arm was a bucket of ice, which held the rum and two glasses.

"Wow," she whispered as Jay set out the impromptu picnic. He didn't seem to hear, so she settled cross-legged on the jetty and reached for a crumbed prawn. She crunched into the morsel. "Oh, that's good."

"Really? I never tried it before. I just asked for something that goes well with rum." Jay perched on the edge of the jetty and dangled his legs over the end. Reaching back, he poured two generous glasses of rum.

Xan took hers and sipped cautiously. Yes, this was Meier's expensive rum. Like burned sugar, searing her throat all the way down as it tasted of fairy floss. She raised her glass. "To the sad stories we need a drink to tell."

Jay snorted, but he drank to her toast. "You really want to know about me and Paige?"

Xan nodded, her mouth too full of lobster to say anything else.

"You won't repeat any of this, right? Romance Island Resort secrets and all? What happens on the island stays on the island?"

Xan nodded again.

"She nearly died because of me. Our first album was rocketing up the charts. We were booking concerts for a tour of the east coast and getting offers to tour the US. I was so busy with the band, I barely had time to see her, so I didn't realise." Jay took a deep draught from his glass. "She showed me the first hate messages, and we laughed about them. Trolls will be trolls, she said. I didn't know she kept on getting them, and how much worse they got. One day, she rocked up at my place. I barely recognised her. I don't think she'd slept for days, and she looked a mess. She barely looked at me as she said we had to end it. Our relationship. I was gutted. It was my first real one, you know? Back then, I knew she was out of my league, or that's what I thought. She was so famous, and I was just some struggling musician." Jay shook his head. "Fuck, look at us now. Six years later. I never thought…"

Xan swallowed the last bit of lobster. "So she dumped you?" She almost laughed, but Jay's grave expression stopped her. "What?"

"Yeah, I guess she did dump me, but I was in love with her. I wanted her to give me another chance. So after a lot to drink, I stumbled over to her place and hammered on the door until she let me in. Fuck, if I'd been a minute later…she had all these pills, lined up on the table, ready to take. I grabbed this big, ugly bowl she had sitting on the table, swept all the pills into it and flushed the lot down the loo. Then I made her tell me everything. Show me everything. All those thousands of fucked-up messages, day in, day out. She got them on social media. They filled up her email inbox and some people had started sending her letters, old-school style, at the studio. They looked like fan mail, but they fucking weren't. She'd stopped going to work because she couldn't face any more of it. So she figured that so many people couldn't be wrong, and she almost…fuck." Jay swiped at his eyes and gave a huge sniff.

Mr Rock Star, crying? Xan kept her eyes on her drink, while Jay got a hold of himself.

"I stayed over that night, but she was adamant. We had to break up, because she couldn't take it any more. If I left her alone, maybe the haters would, too. So I left, making her promise to call me if she so much as thought about suicide again. And she didn't, so I figured she was okay."

Xan's brow furrowed. "But you said your band was on the rise. You were really famous by then, right? If she'd tried to call you, would she have even managed to contact you?"

"Bingo." Jay hunched his shoulders. "I was busy with the band, so I sort of forgot about her. Plenty of girls did want to be with me, so many fans, but I didn't want anyone to have to deal with the sort of attention Paige got, so it was easier just to give the girls one night. One night with a rock star, you know? Something to remember, but too quick for the media to get hold of them. And too many for them to focus on one."

For a moment, Xan wondered if that was Jay's true motivation in his succession of one-night stands. He was famous for them, after all. No one could catch the eligible rock star. In a weird, twisted way, it made a perverse sort of sense. But it wouldn't look that way to the girl he'd left behind.

"What did Paige think of your groupies?" Xan asked.

Jay stared at the waves beneath his feet. "I thought she wouldn't care. After all, she'd said she didn't want me any more. But last night…she said that's what made her try again. Not pills this time. Her wrists. She managed to slice one, but it hurt so much she couldn't go through with it.

She called an ambulance and spent a few days in hospital. That's when her work found out. They didn't know, either, because she hadn't told anyone. Anyone except me, that is." Jay bit down on a prawn.

"What happened then?"

Jay swallowed, then washed the prawn down with a gulp of rum. "They were actually pretty good about it, she said. They took her offscreen and gave her a production job. She was behind the scenes, so no one saw her, and gradually the messages died down. It helped that she didn't have to be on social media any more. She got a PA who dealt with that. She did mostly reality TV, working her way up to production manager. Usually she does cooking shows, but the host of *Farmer Bags A Bride* ended up in rehab, so she agreed to do a season. The network told her it'll be the final season, as the popularity's dropping off, so it's about as low-key as you can get. Normally there's six farmers, but with budget cuts, she only got two. Not that she's complaining. Less work, she said, with only two storylines to set up."

Xan choked on her rum. "Set up? I thought the whole point of reality TV is that it's reality, not scripted!"

Jay laughed. "Oh, it's not scripted. Well, not really. But the show's producers manipulate the people in it, putting them in situations where they're on edge and more likely to snap. They want kisses and tears and outbursts, Paige said. But being a dating show, it's different to the cooking competitions she's done before. She has to invent pressure to put these people under, if competing for the same bachelor isn't enough to do it. Making the blokes line the girls up, then publicly reject one, like one of those shows where people get voted off. Only there's just the bachelor doing the voting, and the girls don't have a say. Not really."

Xan didn't have time for much TV, but she resolved to avoid reality shows like the plague after hearing that. "That's awful."

"Not as bad as the cooking show. When the producer couldn't think of anything else to do, he had one of the techs sabotage some of the appliances, so there'd be an explosion on the show. The company that made it are still trying to get it back, so they can work out what went wrong. She had to smuggle the wreckage home and into her own rubbish bin."

"Was anyone hurt?"

"Nah," Jay replied. "It just made a big mess. And got them a bigger audience for the show, of course. Danger gets them, every time, she said." He drained his glass. "That's why she wanted the show set here. The wildness of the Kimberley, with its crocodiles and tides and huge, isolated stations, instead of the tamed vineyards where they usually host the show. She wanted to do a sort of survivor angle to this show to shake things up a bit, she said. Made me promise not to tell the farmers, though. She wanted to surprise them so she gets genuine reactions when the camera's rolling. Funny. I tried to warn her, but she didn't believe me that the guys were gay. So the surprise was on her."

But Jay and Paige had barely looked at one another yesterday. When had they had time to discuss the show in such depth? "When did she tell you this?" Xan demanded.

"Last night, after a few drinks," Jay drawled, stretching out on the boards. He grinned up at the sky.

Suspicion darkened Xan's thoughts. "You mean you two spent the night together? That's what you meant about what happens on the island, staying on the island? You two hooked up where the media won't find out?" She couldn't keep the disgust out of her tone. He'd slept with Paige hours before agreeing to propose marriage to someone else.

"Nah." Jay didn't sound ruffled. "She wasn't interested. We just drank and talked, really. Catching up. I can survive a night without sex, you know. I think I managed a whole week once."

Xan wasn't sure what to say to that. So she changed the subject. "She's the reason you're doing this, isn't she? You don't really want a wife. You're just doing a girl a favour."

Jay jolted to his feet. "I sure as fuck do want a wife. When I go to Angel's wedding, I won't be going alone. Fuck that for a joke!" He grabbed the rum bottle and swigged from it.

Xan sighed. The arsehole rock star was back with a vengeance. "Thank you for the drink and dinner. I have to work early tomorrow, so I'd best be getting back." She rose, stretched and started back toward the beach.

When she reached the path, she glanced back. Jay stood at the end of the jetty, bottle in hand, muttering. He could take care of himself, she decided, and headed home to bed.

ELEVEN

Penny hunted through every cooking show website she could find, but none of them were calling for entrants at the moment. Frustrated, Penny returned to the site of the show she wanted most. Unlike the others, this wasn't just cooking in front of other chefs. This one was more of a business start-up competition, which made the prize much bigger. *Reign of Restaurants* was its name. The competition started with a massive cook-off, like the others, but the top cooks got to open restaurants in one of the country's capital cities. They got to pick their own menu and serve it to customers for a month, with people voting and reviewing their meals. Sometimes the customers were chefs in disguise, though the cameras kind of gave it away, as there weren't film crews in the restaurant every day.

The restaurant had to host a special banquet for the show's host, Paige, and her team of judges, which got scored. Added to the reviews, ratings and the dollar turnover of the restaurant during the month they were open…and one restaurant would reign supreme, with the show letting the winning cook or cooks have the place. If Penny could get on that programme, and show people just how good she was in the kitchen, she knew she'd be set for life.

But the show didn't seem to be running at the moment, though it would usually start soon. Had the show been cancelled? Or was Paige doing something else now?

Penny feverishly searched for the show's host. Strange. For someone so famous, the woman didn't have much of a social media presence. The most recent reference to her that Penny could find was in relation to a TV dating show.

Penny burst out laughing. Only desperate people went on dating shows. She bet Paige got paid a lot of money to do one of those. She clicked the link to check out the show and a radio announcer's voice boomed out of her speakers: "Could you be the One?"

A muffled voice, slightly distorted, began to describe the qualities of his perfect woman. Not a smoker, of course, making Penny ineligible, but it didn't matter. He wanted a woman who didn't exist and would be way out of his league, even if she did, Penny thought, peering at the video to see what sort of loser they'd duped into being one of the show's bachelors.

Instead of the usual talking head, the video behind the voiceover was dark. Well, not completely dark. There was just enough light to see the bloke's torso, wearing an open, unbuttoned shirt. He was sculpted like a Greek god's statue, too. Now she wondered why a man this hot couldn't get a date.

She watched the video a second time, decided that he probably had a hideously disfigured face, and moved to close the browser entirely.

Then she changed her mind. What if he was some kind of military hero, who'd been injured in action while saving someone else's life? Everyone would be watching the show. If a girl could get on that and show off her cooking skills to both Paige and the world, she'd be a shoe-in for one of the restaurants next time Paige hosted *Reign*.

Penny scanned the page, looking for details on who the man was. Huh. Nothing. The only clue was that he was some sort of celebrity, so the show would be filming at a luxury hotel instead of the usual farms and vineyard.

She'd have to buy nicotine patches and hide them well, if she wanted to make him believe she didn't smoke. Was quitting for a month worth it?

It's not like it'd be the first time. She'd had to quit when she worked at the resort, though she'd started up again since. If it was only for four weeks…

Anything to get her reputation back.

Penny started drafting a letter, telling the studio why she wanted to meet and marry their mystery man.

TWELVE

Paige looked more stressed than she had with the farmers, Jason thought, as he helped her out of the helicopter. What a difference a few weeks made. He wondered how much trouble the network bosses had given her over her proposed changes to the format of the show because of him.

"Are you ready to interview the girls?" she asked. Behind her, the camera crew climbed onto the helipad.

Jason stepped forward to offer his hand, but Paige stopped him.

"As far as you're concerned, they don't exist. They're invisible," she snapped. "I want you to act as natural as possible while we're filming. It's just you and the girls. Ignore my staff."

Reluctantly, Jason lowered his arm and nodded to the crew instead. It wasn't his style to ignore any of his staff at a concert – he knew all the roadies by name when they went on tour. It just didn't feel right. Then again, he'd never done any reality TV before, though he'd had plenty of live interviews. He hoped Paige knew what she was doing.

"Right. Let's go find you a bride," Paige said.

Jason's stomach churned. He hoped she could.

THIRTEEN

They flew in at night, but Penny would have recognised Romance Island Resort anyway. She'd worked there for a season, after all. Even after working on a cruise ship, the resort was still what she thought of when someone talked about luxury accommodation. Even the biggest suites on the ship couldn't compare to the Pearl Villas at Romance Island Resort.

Not that she got to stay in a villa. Penny and the other girls were shepherded into the hotel proper, and given standard rooms. They were told to get a good night's sleep and make themselves look good for a meet and greet first thing in the morning, where they'd be interviewed about their hopes for the show.

Penny had watched a few reality shows in her time, so she knew the film crew took soundbites from the interviews to use later on in the season, usually completely out of context. So if you mentioned something you hated or said something controversial, you could expect it to come up on the show at some point. The trick was to say something the viewers liked and remembered, like Mystery Man with his talk about the One. She'd heard the girls at the Roey repeating the video verbatim, wishing they were brave enough or single enough to enter the race for him. She hadn't been game to tell them that she had – or that she'd been one of the lucky few to receive an invitation to actually meet him. Broome being the small town it was, rumours were flying about which hotel he was staying at, seeing as most of the places in town had been asked to sponsor a date with him, so they knew he was here. Hell, they could be serving him lunch right now, and they'd never even know it was him!

But it all felt much more real when she woke up in the cushy hotel room. She had to dress up and do her makeup for the first day of filming. Funny, she'd expected the show to at least have a makeup artist, but maybe there were too many of them to deal with on the same day.

Knowing the Broome weather better than most, she chose light cotton pants and a nice shirt. The resort had beautiful beaches and anything more formal would look ridiculous among the palm trees and white sand. She stuck her cleanest pair of thongs on her feet and made her way to the Jungle, the resort's pub.

This early in the day, it wasn't open yet, but that hadn't stopped Paige. She bustled around, telling the camera crew and resort staff how to set things up exactly like she wanted them.

A bunch of other girls clustered around a coffee pot and

a platter of pastries. Penny's growling stomach insisted she go join them, and she didn't argue. The coffee was too hot to taste and the pastries were sweet enough to spike her blood sugar, she soon found, breathing an inward sigh of relief.

As she sipped her coffee, she took stock of the competition. She hadn't expected so many. She counted ten, besides herself, when one more girl walked into the room.

"Oh, this will be a piece of cake," the blonde newcomer said, curling her painted lip. She'd been shoehorned into a short dress that wouldn't have been out of place in a strip club, except for the overabundance of ruffles that helped it cross the borderline into decency. She must have used a whole roll of that Hollywood tape to stop her boobs from falling out, too. Penny hoped it hurt when she had to take it all off.

She wasn't the only blonde, or the only one dressed slutty. But the blondes were outnumbered by the brunettes, and there was even a redhead. There were short girls and average height girls like herself, ranging right up to the statuesque, sneering blonde, though her heels definitely gave her height a boost. No, Mystery Man hadn't chosen the girls based on physical preferences, unless there was something Penny had missed.

Paige clapped her hands for their attention. "Right, girls! Everyone had their coffee? Good, because we have a long day of filming ahead! First, we're going to do your entry sequence."

That meant filming them while they walked up the path to the pub, shaking Paige's hand and exchanging air kisses, before taking their place in a circle of bar stools. She made them do it three times, despite the whining from girls with heels that hurt to walk in. Next, she had her assistant take them in groups down to the beach, where she had them filmed walking along the sand. The groups who remained were taken one by one to what Penny liked to think of as interrogation booths.

She had to sit on a stool under a bright spotlight and answer question after question, sometimes more than once, and she swore the interviewer lost her place and repeated herself. Penny tried to keep her patience, though, and hoped she gave the same response each time. It was hard to keep track, especially with the rapid fire questions. Her hopes for the show. How she'd feel if she won Mystery Man's heart. What she liked most about him so far. What chance she thought she had now she'd seen the other girls. Which girl she thought would win. Her top guesses for Mystery Man's identity. Her idea of the perfect man. Whether she thought Mystery Man would measure up.

She answered as best she could, especially when the questions were downright stupid. Of course she didn't know who he was, or much about him at all, so she made stuff up, hoping it sounded good. The third time she was asked about his identity, she listed a bunch of superheroes, hoping it would be the last time she heard that question. The interviewer's poker face gave away nothing, though.

By the time filming was finished, the bar was open, and Penny was deeply in need of a drink. And a smoke, of course, but she wasn't allowed that, so alcohol would have to do.

"How much is your cheapest pint?" Penny asked the

barman, hoping she had enough.

"For you, free. She's paying." The barman pointed at Paige.

Penny sighed and pulled her wallet off the counter.

"Oh, while you have that out, you may as well show me your ID. Just to prove you're old enough for beer," the barman said. "If you look under 25 and all…"

Penny nodded wearily and slid her driver's licence across the counter.

"Get me a glass of champagne," an imperious voice ordered.

Penny didn't need to look. It was the blonde bitch from this morning.

"Show me your ID, then," the barman said, handing back Penny's. He then completely ignored the card the bitch thrust at him to ask Penny, "So which beer did you say you wanted again?"

Penny pointed at the tap marked with one of the boutique beers from the local brewery, one she'd never been able to afford. If she didn't like it, it wouldn't matter, seeing as she wasn't paying for it.

As she took her beer, she glanced at the other girl's ID, trying to read the name so she wouldn't have to ask. The girl's perfectly painted claws covered half of it, though, so Penny gave up and sipped her beer. Oh, it was good. She hoped she'd have time for another one before Paige sent them all back to their rooms for the night.

The shortest brunette walked up to the bar. While the barman brought her soft drink, she stuck out a hand to Penny. "I'm Calais," she said.

"Penelope," Penny said, shaking the girl's hand.

Calais turned to the blonde bitch, who eyed her coldly like something that had stuck to her stiletto.

"I'm Lorelei, and I'm going to win this. You two don't have a chance of making it through the first round of interviews, dressed like that, so excuse me if I don't bother remembering your names." She swept away with her drink.

Penny frowned. That hadn't been the name on the girl's licence. She hadn't read it that clearly, but there'd been no Ls. Maybe the bitch was some sort of minor celebrity herself, and Lorelei was her stage name.

Calais sucked on the straw of her soda. "So, do you think she's a stripper, a hooker or a model?"

Penny laughed. "With that dress, she could be all three."

FOURTEEN

Penny thought she was prepared for the speed-dating interview with Mystery Man, but when she found herself pushed into a dark room, she panicked. A spotlight clicked on, blinding her.

"Sit down, please, Penelope."

Penny thought his voice sounded familiar. One of the cameramen from yesterday? Maybe. She couldn't be sure which one, as Paige had instructed them to relax and ignore the camera crew as much as possible. Easy for her to say, Penny thought. Paige wasn't sitting on a stool under a spotlight, expecting to be interrogated by some military type who lurked in the shadows, unseen.

His questions weren't barked the way the other interviewers had done. No, he drawled them slowly, his sexy voice lulling her to relax. God, that voice…where had she heard it before?

"So what would you say is your best feature, Penelope?" he purred.

She took a moment to remind herself that she was here to cook, not let the man melt her insides like chocolate fondue. "I'm a genius in the kitchen," she said, then decided to add, "And not just with food, either. You know how they say if you can't stand the heat, you should get out of the kitchen? Well, I love the heat. And if you come into my kitchen, I'll take your tastebuds on a tour more tantalising than anything you've ever imagined."

He chuckled. "That sounds awesome. I might have to take you up on that."

It clicked. She did know him! That voice, she'd heard it murmur in her ear when she'd given in to that rock star. Oh, what was his name? She'd forgotten. Not the sex, though. She remembered that. No one forgot that mindblowing, melt-your-undies sort of sex. The sort you wanted so much more of, but never got, because men like him didn't choose girls like her. They ended up with models like Lorelei, who didn't deserve any of what the universe handed to them on a platter.

She was so busy daydreaming, she missed his next question. Mortified, she asked him to repeat it.

"What's your idea of the perfect date, Penelope?"

Her mind went blank. "I...I don't know," she stammered. "I think I'd like to leave that up to the guy who asked me out. And if he made sure I had a really good time, the morning after, I'd cook him a breakfast fit for a rock star." Oh, fuck! She held her breath, hoping he hadn't realised she knew who he was. Well, sort of. She still couldn't remember his name.

She breathed a sigh of relief as he launched into the next question, hoping the interrogation would end soon.

FIFTEEN

Penny escaped to the bar as soon as Mystery Man was done with her. It wasn't that she wanted to get away from him as much as…the mortification of some of the stupid things she'd said. She'd tried to be funny, replying with a Simpsons joke, and while she thought he'd understood the reference at the time, now she worried that it made her look childish for referring to a kids' cartoon. Rock stars didn't watch cartoons.

In the Jungle, she could hear loud, female voices bragging about all the celebrities they'd met and shagged. Loudest of all was a girl who claimed that she'd even slept with billionaire Gaia Vasse, and how she'd be willing to do a threesome with Mystery Man and anyone he wanted. Smugly, she added, "I told him so, too. He sounded impressed."

"I told him I give the best blowjobs this side of the

equator, and I offered to show him right there in the interview. I think if the cameras hadn't been on, he'd have done it, too," another voice piped up.

"I said I'd be a perfectly obedient wife, fulfilling his every wish, and if I didn't, he could tie me up and spank me," a third proclaimed proudly.

Penny peeped around the palm trees and caught sight of the little group. Perfectly made-up model types, the lot of them. Like Lorelei. Nothing like herself. Penny was as common as they came, talking about cooking and cartoons, when she should have been offering him wild, gourmet sex instead. She was so stupid. She'd never make it past the first round. Cooking for him on TV? Dream on, girl, she told herself. She'd be back waitressing at the Roey before she could blink, while these girls serviced him every moment the cameras weren't watching. What hope did she have against women like that?

SIXTEEN

Jason tried not to yawn as the fifth girl described whatever she'd seen on the porn channel last night in excruciating detail. Where had they gotten the idea he wanted them to talk about sex? Talk was boring. He was more a man of action, himself.

"How many more have I got left to go?" he asked the cameraman when Porn Fan Number Five had left.

"Just one. Callie, I think her name is."

A moment later, the shortest girl of the lot crept into the room and climbed onto the spotlit stool. Between her slumped shoulders and downcast eyes, Jason wondered why the girl was so miserable.

"Welcome, Callie, to your CIA-sponsored speed date," he quipped. "I'm just going to ask you a few questions and —"

She raised her head. "It's Calais, actually." Her voice was

surprisingly firm.

"Like the city?" he asked.

It was her turn to look surprised. "Most Aussie blokes think I was named after the Holden car. Neither, actually. My family's Greek and Mum wanted her kids to have names that were a bit different. So she picked names she liked from some of the ancient stories."

Xan and her talk of quests. Now he couldn't stop thinking about it and this girl's name was too much of a coincidence for him to ignore.

"So this Calais character you're named after. Was she some virginal maiden who became some hero's incredibly faithful and obedient wife? Or did she just get seduced by some god or other?" Jason would put his money on the second one, but she'd surprised him once. It could be the first one.

Calais laughed. "Neither, actually. Calais was a man. A hero who went off questing with Hercules and his mates, but Hercules killed him because Hercules' lover didn't survive a battle while Calais did. You're thinking of Penelope, Odysseus' faithful wife, who didn't remarry while he was away at the siege of Troy and taking the long way home afterwards. You've got one of those here, too."

"A faithful wife?"

"No, a Penelope. I met her on the first night. She's nice. Funny, too."

Jason glanced down at his list of questions, moving on to the first one. He'd had enough of sitting in this stuffy, dark room. He wanted to make his choice and get on with the show.

SEVENTEEN

"They're ready for you, Mr Felix," Allie, Paige's assistant said.

Why did he suddenly feel so nervous? It wasn't like he was proposing already. Jason had watched everyone's interview videos again today, to ensure sure he was making the right decision. The porn girls he dismissed immediately, which left seven. He was only supposed to choose six, though, which meant one had to go. Four of them he'd genuinely liked. They'd been easy choices.

The other three, though…model material, all with an eye for the camera. The sort of girl a rock star was expected to have on his arm at events, though he never had before. Any of these three would warrant a media splash that would put Gaia's fake engagement into the box of lies where it belonged.

Gaia. One of them had mentioned Gaia, thinking he'd

be impressed. Actually, he'd struggled not to gag. He'd manfully managed one night with the billionaire, but he couldn't summon the slightest bit of enthusiasm for another. Especially not with another girl watching. Besides, if he sent the girl back to Gaia, they both might leave him alone.

There. Decision made. He had his list of six. Now he just needed to remember it while the cameras were rolling and everyone was looking to him to make his choice.

He hitched up his best cheeky grin and waited on the Jungle veranda, winking occasionally at the camera.

"And now, I'd like to properly introduce our mysterious bachelor, Mr…"

"GO!" Allie mouthed.

Jason sauntered up the steps.

"…JAY FELIX!" Paige finished, clapping loudly with all the girls.

She'd lined them up, like they did to criminals at a police station.

Jason felt an overwhelming urge to say, "Yes, officer, that's the girl who said she'd deep-throat my dick while fisting herself." Except that he'd have to point the finger at five of them, and Paige would get pissed off because she couldn't show that on TV, so he'd have to go back out and start over. It'd be worth it, though, to see the shock on their faces…

At least they all looked delighted to find out that he was the bachelor to their brides-to-be. That was enough to keep his grin in place while he chose not to cause any more trouble than necessary.

"Have you chosen your six favourites?" Paige asked.

"Yes, Paige, I have."

"Well, let's hear their names, then!"

Jason cleared his throat. "First, I have to say what amazing women they all are. Coming all the way out here, not knowing who I am..." He drivelled on for the required five minutes until he caught Paige's slight nod. Good. He'd talked up the girls enough so that the ones who left wouldn't look too bad, and he didn't look overeager to get started.

Think of it as foreplay, Paige had said. Spin it out until they're so close they're ready to scream, and then give them a little. And a little bit more...

Yeah, he got the picture. He wondered how many bachelors she'd said that to, and realised this was the only dating show she'd done. So she absolutely knew what she was asking for, when she suggested he pretend this was foreplay. He could take all damn night if he wanted to.

"The first favourite I choose is...Calais."

She beamed, crossed the room to hug Paige, and then gave him a hug, too, before standing by his side. On the other side of the room a few smug smiles had turned to looks of consternation. Good.

"The second one...will be Maia."

Panic had set in among the porn fans.

Jason waited until Maia had finished her hugs before he took a deep breath and said, "My third favourite is...Daphne."

The girl emitted an ear-splitting screech, then insisted on hugging everybody. Jason watched with smug satisfaction as the remaining girls in line wore forced smiles as they awkwardly returned Daphne's hugs.

"The fourth one is…Lorelei."

Tall and proud, this girl strutted to his side of the room, joining the line of girls without deigning to hug anyone.

He glimpsed Allie's signal and remembered the next bit of drivel he'd promised to deliver. "It was really hard to choose only six of these wonderful women, and I'd like to thank…"

He only droned on for two minutes this time, cutting the speech short because he wanted to put the remaining girls out of their misery. This was cruel.

"My fifth favourite is…Melissa!"

The redhead tossed her head and marched across the room, choosing to give him a hug, but not Paige. Paige didn't seem put out, so Jason took a deep breath to end this performance.

And his mind went blank. Staring at the girl with ebony-coloured hair, who was looking at the floor, he completely forgot her name. The *Simpsons* fan who'd looked the most animated when she was talking about cooking. C'mon, her name had to be in his head somewhere…

"Penelope," someone breathed beside him.

He glanced left to find Calais grinning up at him. She nodded toward the same girl.

"And the sixth and final girl I choose to spend the next four weeks with, here in the Kimberley, is…Penelope!"

EIGHTEEN

Penny's breath hissed out in relief as he said her name. She truly hadn't believed he'd pick her and now…and now…

She opened her eyes to find Paige beckoning her silently to move to where the other chosen girls stood. Oh, right. She didn't want to stand with the rejects any longer than she had to. Not so confident now, were they? The cheap tarts who'd boasted so casually about screwing celebrities in the pub weren't going to get their claws in Jay.

But Penny might. If she was really, really lucky.

She didn't want the man, she wanted the opportunity to cook for him, she reminded herself, but it was no use. For just a moment, she let her imagination run riot, that she'd won the competition, and Jay would be hers. If only…

"Well, that was kind of him," Lorelei said, startling Penny into opening her eyes again. "Or perhaps unkind, depending on your perspective."

"What do you mean?" demanded Daphne.

"Well, he had to choose five other girls after me, because it's part of the show rules. So he sent away the girls who might have given me some competition, and gave the rest of you false hope. Now it's MY turn to be kind." She stuck her hands on her hips. "Forget it. He's mine. Give up hope now, because you don't have a chance."

Daphne opened her mouth to protest, but she couldn't seem to find the right words. Melissa just looked disgusted, while Maia rolled her eyes. Calais fixed her gaze firmly on the floor and Penny bunched her hands into fists.

"How would you know?" Penny spat. "He chose all of us. That gives you one chance in six. No better than the rest of us."

Lorelei looked her up and down. "Oh, I am better than the rest of you. And if you don't see it, you're delusional."

Penny drew back her fist.

"Oh good, you're all still here," Paige said.

Grudgingly, Penny dropped her hands to her sides.

"Now the show really gets started," Paige continued. "Once the other girls are gone, I'd like you to return to your rooms and pack your things, too. We'll spend one more night here before we head out in the morning to your new home for the next four weeks. Well, those of you who are lucky enough to stay for the full four weeks. Not all of you will, by the way. But that's the price you pay, when the prize is a rock star's heart. And what a chest it's in, right, girls?"

No one responded.

"We'll do a quick set of video interviews with each of you, asking how you feel about our bachelor, now you know who he is. Now's the time to really spill your feelings, because Jay will be with us at our new home. I just can't wait! Can you?"

"Where are we going?" Melissa asked.

Paige clapped her hands. "The home of romance, of course!"

NINETEEN

By the next morning, Paige still hadn't been any more forthcoming. "Get in, girls. Leave your gear on the jetty – Luke will come back for that next trip!" Paige cried, gesturing at the jet boat as if it was a luxury yacht and not one of the pearl farm's battered dive boats.

Penny and the other girls trooped aboard. Well, all of them except Lorelei, who stood on the jetty, squawking about how she was afraid of boats.

Stay on land all alone then, Penny thought but didn't say.

"Nothing to be afraid of. There won't be any whirlpools in the Sound for hours, if you go now," Jay remarked, scooping Lorelei up.

She squealed in delight, but her triumph was short-lived as Jay took three steps, then set her down on the side of the boat.

"My shoe!" she screeched.

Penny peered over the side. Sure enough, she could see one of Lorelei's ridiculously high heels sinking into the milky, blue water.

"These are Jimmy Choos!" Lorelei wailed. "You have to get it!"

Penny recognised the name of the Malaysian shoe designer whose wares she'd never be able to afford, and prayed silently that no one surrendered to Lorelei's pleas. The bitch deserved to lose her expensive shoes. She could probably afford to buy a new pair every week.

The boat pulled away from the jetty, amid Lorelei's wails of what she was supposed to do with only one shoe.

Daphne dealt with the problem. She leaned over, ripped off Lorelei's other shoe and pitched it over the side of the boat. "There. Now the fish can have a matching pair."

Everyone except Lorelei laughed.

"Wait, what about Jay?" Maia asked, pointing.

Jay stood on the jetty, his chiselled chest and abs gleaming in the sun, as he waved to them.

Luke shrugged. "He's headed over on my next trip, when I bring the gear. We have to set up camp first. Something rock stars don't have to do." He sounded bitter. Jealous, maybe.

Who wouldn't be? Every girl's gaze was fixed on the rock god. The bloke driving the boat didn't exist to them with Jay around.

For a moment, Penny dared to hope that Jay could be hers. Every inch of hard muscle, hers to have any time she wanted. Not just once. Her mouth went dry. It was like winning the lottery. No, better than that. But not for her.

Never for her. The universe hated her. She'd never have someone like Jay. Better to focus on what she was really here for – to showcase her cooking on television, so she could finish her apprenticeship and open her own restaurant. Where she could cook what she wanted, without some overbearing bloke telling her what to do, and people would come from all over the country, no, all over the world, just to taste…

"He looks so yummy, doesn't he?" Calais' soft words dragged Penny out of her daydream. "I still can't believe I'm here. A month with him sounds like a dream, though I don't think I'll last that long."

"What do you mean?" Penny asked.

"Well, we won't all get to stay for the whole time. We get eliminated. Voted off the island, sort of. Except Jay's the one who has to choose who stays and who goes." Calais bowed her head. "I bet I'm the first to go."

Penny surveyed the mousy girl, who probably had a point. From what she remembered, Jay liked his girls outspoken and confident. "I hope it's Lorelei. Shit, I wish she'd fallen over the side instead of her shoes." She glanced up, hoping the cameraman hadn't heard that. No, he didn't even have his camera on. It hung by his side, pointed at the deck.

Calais laughed. "I liked her shoes. I could never walk in them, of course, but they were pretty. Not something you'd want to wear out here, though." She kicked her sneakers against the side of the boat.

Penny glanced down at the thongs on her feet. "No."

The cameraman swore and rushed to the side, camera in hand.

"What is it?" Maia called.

"There's a pod of dolphins over by the oyster lines. Feeding, by the look of it." Luke pointed at some black buoys.

Penny squinted at the water, and something broke the surface, then slipped under again. Could be a dolphin, but could be a shark, too. Plenty of them around here.

"And there's home for the next four weeks. Shenton Bluff." Luke pointed proudly at a row of what looked like tents, lined up along the beach.

"We're sleeping in those?" Daphne whined. "I thought we were staying at the resort! There might be bugs!"

Penny hoped there would be bugs. Big, deadly, venomous ones that wanted whiny bitch for breakfast.

"Nope, you're not sleeping in those. Your tents are by the fire pit. You have to assemble them yourselves."

Lorelei's wailing drowned out Daphne's.

Luke raised his voice so he could be heard over the two idiots. "First one finished doesn't have to cook tonight, and the last one to finish has to do the dishes." The boat ground to a halt in the shallows, a good twenty metres from shore. "Go get them, girls!"

TWENTY

Penny didn't hesitate. She slipped over the side, landing knee-deep in the warm ocean. She trudged through the shallows to shore.

"You have to take one of the tent kits to a platform, and when you're finished, it has to look like that one there!" Luke shouted. Penny's eyes followed the direction of his outstretched arm until she found the tent in question.

Huh. She'd expected the tents to be complicated, but they were the same as the heavy-duty four-man safari tents she'd used at every school camp. One person could put them up, even if that person was a ten-year-old who wasn't listening to a word her teacher said. The hardest bit was banging the pegs into the ground if it was rocky, or you couldn't find something suitable to use as a hammer.

Penny grabbed a kit and hauled it up to the platform furthest from the beach — and beside the only proper building at the campsite. When she grew close enough to read the signs, she congratulated herself on her foresight. The rainwater tanks were a big hint, as were the doors lined up along one side, but the signs identifying it as the toilet and bathroom block sealed the deal. She wasn't wandering around in the dark through the camp when she needed to go to the loo.

She emptied her bag on the raised decking. Tent, centre pole…but no pegs! Swearing, she dropped to her knees and searched the bag for them, but the tent pegs were nowhere to be seen. She'd have to head back to the fire pit and see if another kit had spares. Penny stomped across the decking, annoyed at whoever had forgotten to pack her tent kit properly, she didn't notice the metal ring until she caught her toe in it. Too late to correct, she sprawled onto the sand dune, getting a face full of sand.

Shrieks of laughter floated up from the fire pit. The other girls had reached the tents just in time to see her face-plant. Swearing some more, Penny dragged herself back onto the platform to rip out whatever had tripped her.

Sure enough, there was a metal ring, firmly fixed to the platform, with a clinking carabiner clipped to it. But it looked like it was supposed to be there.

Maybe the reason there weren't any pegs was because she didn't need any, Penny mused, unfolding her tent so the base spread across the platform. She pulled one of the peg loops over to the metal ring and clipped them together with the carabiner. Crawling across the platform, she did the same with the other tent corners. Much easier than hammering pegs into hardened clay, and much sturdier than shifting beach sand.

All she had to do was put up the centre pole, throw the fly over and tie that down. Easy.

"Whoever's tent goes up first doesn't have to cook!" Luke bellowed, striding along the path to the bathrooms. "You'll get to relax with us blokes by the fire pit!"

Except…Penny didn't want to be first. She wanted to cook in front of the cameras. That's what she was here for.

She surveyed the other girls. Calais had picked the platform next to hers, and she was unfolding her tent with a bewildered look on her face. On the next platform, Maia and Melissa were puzzling over a sheet of instructions that had come with one of their tents. The two closest to the fire pit had been claimed by the whiners, Lorelei and Daphne. Lorelei had managed to drag her bag up the dune, by virtue of her bare feet, but Daphne's heels kept sinking into the sand, and she refused to remove them.

She had to help someone else come first. Not Lorelei or Daphne, and the two Ms were already allies. That left quiet Calais. If she was first, she'd be too shy to talk to Jay or even Luke. Penny's decision was made.

"Have you ever put up a tent before?" Penny addressed Calais.

Calais shook her head. "I've been camping plenty of times, but we never bothered with a tent. We just threw the swags in the back of the ute and strung up a tarp if we needed it to shelter from the dew. Tents are for townies and tourists."

Penny gritted her teeth. "Well, how about letting this townie show you what to do?"

"Please," Calais said fervently.

With two of them clipping and tying, they had the tent

up in minutes.

"And Penny's first!" Luke roared.

"No, I'm not!" Penny shouted back frantically. "This is Calais's tent. Mine's that one." She pointed at the staked tent lying on her platform. Scrambling through the scrub to hers, she screwed the centre pole together and used it to raise the roof. Next, she shook out the fly and tried to flip it over the top of the tent. The breeze caught it and blew it back in her face. "Shit."

Someone peeled it away from her. "Let me help. After all, you helped me." Calais offered a smile as she took two corners of Penny's flysheet. Together, they hoisted it over the tent and tied the corners down.

"First is Calais, second is Penny! Who will be next?" Luke yelled, sounding like a carnival barker at the Royal Show.

"Who cares?" Penny muttered.

"Bedrolls are on the decking outside the kitchen," a female voice said. "That big tent at the end. The one that looks like a canvas donga. That's the kitchen."

Penny and Calais glanced up in surprise.

A woman, dressed in a uniform similar to Luke's, stood on the bathroom block veranda. "Hi, I'm Bec," she said. "When he's done ordering you around, he'll tell you about the bedding. I'll tell you a secret, though. The ones with the best mattresses will have names written on them, because the tour guides claim them. See if you can get Luke's before he does."

"But leave yours alone?" Calais asked.

Bec shrugged. "All the tents are taken. I'll be sleeping in one of the tent cabins tonight. They've all got beds with linen for the glamping crowd, so I won't need a swag."

"Why don't we get beds?" Penny asked.

"You'd have to ask the TV crew that. They booked you into the tents. Maybe their budget doesn't run to more than that." Bec nodded toward the two Ms. "You better hurry. It looks like those two are nearly done with theirs."

Calais and Penny collected their bedding and lugged it up to their tents, then headed back to the fire pit, where Bec now sat in a plastic garden chair.

"Grab yourself a beer," Bec said, pointing with hers. "The local brewery's sponsoring the show, so there's plenty."

"No, I need these two for interviews," Paige chimed in, linking her arms through Penny's and Calais'. "Show me your little canvas palaces, girls, and tell the viewers your secret. How did you get it up so fast?"

Penny summoned a smile for the camera as she forced out a laugh at Paige's innuendo. "Oh, experience. I had lots of practice back home."

"Oh really?" Paige purred. "Do tell!"

Penny launched into a story about every school camp and outdoor education camp-out she could remember, leaving out the times she'd shared a tent with Craig Davies, even under the teachers' watchful eyes. Of course, that was before he'd hooked up with that complete skank Kristen, and dumped her at the school social in front of everyone.

She'd gotten her revenge, though. She'd managed to get a garden hose that reached from the outside tap to Kristen's locker. Then she'd sealed the locker with electrical tape and filled it with bore water on a hot Friday afternoon. By the time Kristen opened it on Monday morning, the locker had been absolutely rank. She'd had to throw all her books out, they'd reeked so badly. And her iPod, which she'd left in there over the weekend by accident.

"And how about you, Callie?" Paige asked.

"It's Calais," the girl corrected, reddening.

"Of course. Have you done a lot of camping, Calais?"

Calais stared at her feet. "I grew up on a farm. My brother and sister and I camped out at the creek a fair bit, growing up. When we were younger, we took horses down to the pool at the bottom of the waterfall, but when we got older, we'd all pile into one of the utes and take it up the coast so we could camp on the beach. But now – "

"That's not fair! You cheated!" Daphne screeched. "They had help, and you cheated!"

"Not my fault you're slow," Lorelei taunted, skipping down the dune as Luke finished tying her flysheet for her. He moved to help Daphne next.

"I'm not doing the dishes!" Daphne continued. "I'll ruin my nails."

While Paige wasn't looking, Calais slipped away into the bathroom block. Penny hid a triumphant smile. This was too easy. Lorelei and Daphne wouldn't last long, and Calais was too shy to want much camera time.

"I should go see if I can do anything for dinner," Penny said.

"You should've been first. Why did you stop to help the other girl?" Paige asked.

Penny glanced at the camera, which was firmly fixed on her. "She needed help, and we're all in this together, you know? Besides, I like cooking. I'm training to be a chef. I don't want to sit around doing nothing while someone else burns dinner. That's my passion."

"Not Jay Felix?"

Penny forced herself to laugh. "And him, of course. But you know, the way to a man's heart is through his stomach. Jay Felix might be a rock star, but he's still a man. Have you seen those washboard abs?"

Paige gestured to the cameraman to stop filming, to Penny's relief. "Damn, it's hot here. I need a drink." Paige said.

"Me, too," Penny replied, following her to the kitchen.

TWENTY-ONE

Jason rode in the bow of the jet boat, letting the fresh sea air cool his foggy head. So many girls and so much to remember. Their names, for a start. He scanned the shore, testing his memory with the people he saw. The little one sitting beside the fire pit was Calais from Katanning. Emerging from the nearest tent was the statuesque blonde. Lorelei, her name was. He couldn't remember where she was from. The curviest one was Maia, and the redhead was Melissa. Where were the other two?

The boat keel grated on the sand, and Jason took that as his cue to jump into the water.

"Your bag, Mr Felix." Baz handed it to him.

Jason nodded his thanks, slung the bag over his shoulder and splashed to shore. Paige met him with a big smile for the camera trailing behind her.

"Welcome to Camp Romance!" she trilled.

Jason couldn't help himself. He burst out laughing. The blokes at the pearl farm would pitch a fit at the new name for Shenton Camp. Come to think of it, so would the tour company who used the place. He had to get a hold of himself. With considerable effort, Jason swallowed back the rest of his laughter and tried to keep a straight face. "Thanks."

Paige's fixed smile didn't waver. "Let me show you to your oceanside cabin, Jay." She trudged along the sand track and Jason had no choice but to follow her.

Six years and she'd barely changed a bit. Paige had always had a fine, pert, little arse, which her shorts showed off nicely. There wasn't much Jason regretted about his past, but breaking up with Paige was one of those exceptions. He wished they could have done things differently, somehow, to save Paige from all the pain she'd gone through because of him, but it was too late for that now. What was done was done, and no amount of perving on her now would change that. She might as well be as distant as the moon; he'd never be able to touch her again. She didn't want the media baggage that came with him.

Would any of these girls want it? Flavia hadn't. She'd cursed him for it, too, even though Gaia had unleashed that particular media storm. But this was different. All the girls at Camp Romance had signed up to be seen with him on TV. They wanted the attention, or at least they'd agreed to it. Maybe this was how he should have done things in the first place.

Let the public warm up to the woman in his life before he declared their relationship to the world. Social media could go wild with rumours and predictions, while they watched love blossom, or at least the beginning of it. Four weeks wasn't long enough to fall in love.

Angel did, his traitorous mind reminded him. She'd vanished, reappeared and woken up from her coma in the space of four short weeks, only to fall for that psycho. The one she was going to marry in a matter of months.

"You don't look happy," Paige observed, peering through the door of Jason's cabin.

Cabin was a generous word for it. It was just a bigger tent than the ones the girls slept in, with canvas draped over a sturdier metal frame bolted to the concrete floor. Like one of those marquees he'd played in when it rained at outdoor concert venues. There were two single beds inside the cabin, instead of a stage, though.

"Who am I sharing with?" he asked.

"Nobody, or at least, not yet." Paige winked for the ever-present camera. "Each girl has her own tent, just like you get your own cabin. I'm at the opposite end, and the ones in between will sleep my camera crew and the tour company staff." She pointed up the slope to a wooden structure. "That's the bathroom, and the kitchen's at the other end. It's not Romance Island Resort, but the view's to die for."

She was right about the view. If you angled your head just right, the canvas was almost transparent, like it wasn't there at all, and you could see clear across King Sound. Not to the Buccaneer Archipelago, of course, which was hidden around the eastern headland, but that only added to the feeling of isolation. When all this was over, Jason wanted to come back here for a week with a few of his guitars and just chill. There was just something about this place…

A shriek shattered the peace. "Where's my bedding? My bags are here, but nothing else. Where am I supposed to sleep?"

Paige swore, then glanced at Jason. "What? It doesn't matter if the cameras are rolling. We'll edit that out, or bleep it, if we have to." She hurried toward the fire pit, where it looked like one of the girls was having the mother of all tantrums.

Jason wracked his brain to remember her name as he trailed behind Paige. The shrieking harpy wasn't his problem, so he hung back, watching. Daphne, that was it.

From her ear-splitting tirade, he learned that someone hadn't brought enough swags for all the campers, and she'd missed out. Baz and his boat were gone, and no one's mobile phone had any reception out here.

The girl wouldn't shut up, though almost everyone in the camp surrounded her, offering her all sorts of things to placate her. All except one. A woman Jason didn't know sat on the kitchen veranda, her expression mirroring his disgust at the girl's performance.

Jason sat beside the woman. "I don't think we've met." He extended a hand. "Jay Felix."

She laughed shortly and shook his hand. "I know you, Mr Felix. I'm Bec. It's nice to meet you." She jerked her head at the fire pit. "More than I can say for some. There were enough swags. I counted them myself. Someone's hidden one, and my money's on him." She pointed at the man wearing a uniform that matched hers.

"I'd put my money on the TV crew, personally," Jay replied. "Trying to create drama for the show."

Bec shook her head. "Nah, it's just him being a dick.

We've got cabins, but he insists on sleeping under the stars with a swag. Should've brought his own, but he didn't, so he took one of the company's. He won't admit it, though. Stubborn git."

Jason rose. "Which cabin's his?"

"Third one along." Bec pointed.

"Time for a hero to save the day, then." Jay hitched up a grin and strode into the midst of the mob. "What's this? A lady without a bed?"

Daphne opened her mouth to repeat her sob story.

"Can't have that," he continued quickly. "I'd be happy to keep you warm tonight, to make up for any mistakes that have been made."

Jason found himself surrounded by shocked and horrified expressions. Even Daphne's, though hers quickly morphed into triumph.

"All right, then," she said grudgingly.

"Follow me," he said, leading the way to Cabin Number Three. He waved her in and smothered a grin when she closed the door behind them. Jason crossed the floor to one of the metal lockers that contained linen in his cabin. Pulling out an armload of the stuff, he foisted it on her. "There. That should be enough. It won't be that cold a night." Nodding with satisfaction, he walked back to the veranda, whistling.

All eyes were on him, and Jason recognised the sort of awe he usually got for being a rock star instead of a harpy-wrangler. Well, he was that, too. He addressed the crowd, "Now, I want a beer."

He'd need a lot more before this was over. This reality TV business was a lot harder than he thought it'd be.

TWENTY-TWO

Penny did everything she could to make cooking look artistic, but even she had to admit there wasn't much she could do with sauce-out-of-a-jar spaghetti bolognaise. She just didn't have the ingredients to play with that would make it special. Not that it mattered, really – the cameraman kept his case clipped shut the whole time she was cooking.

More than once, she glanced over at Calais, sitting primly on her seat beside Jay. The other girls did various chores, stacking wood for the fire, preparing the salad and setting out the plates and cutlery for the meal, but Calais had earned the coveted spot by having her tent ready first.

Destiny had dumped on her again, Penny fumed. She should've been first, and not helped at all, seeing as no one was recording her culinary skills.

Jay leaned in and spoke to Calais, but the girl didn't react at all.

Penny smothered a laugh. In the gathering dusk, Jay evidently hadn't noticed her earbuds. Calais had her iPod clenched in one hand, playing music that drowned out anything he said.

Dinner didn't take long, so she dished up. She felt slightly mollified when the camera came out just in time to record everyone complimenting her on the delicious meal. Even Jay, who had his mouth full at the time. She hoped they showed that bit of footage when the show went to air. An endorsement from a rock star who was used to Michelin starred cuisine was quite the compliment.

Daphne whined and complained about having to do the dishes, but she quietened down after Luke said he'd come in and give her a hand.

Penny picked at her salad, still eating long after everyone else had finished. The sound of plates crashing around in the sink had ceased by the time she was done, so she slipped into the dimly lit kitchen to wash her own plate, figuring she was too late to avail herself of Daphne's dishwashing services.

A moan from the darkness stopped her dead. As her eyes adjusted, Penny realised she could see a shape beside the bench at the far end of the kitchen. No, not one shape – two, joined at the hip, humping on the bench.

"Oh, harder," Daphne begged. "I've dreamed about being with a rock star."

Penny fought down bile. The first night here, and she was already banging Jay? Was that what he wanted, someone who had sex at the slightest whim, where anyone could see them? Jealousy churned in her belly.

But Penny didn't want Jay now, she reminded herself.

She wanted to cook on live TV, that was all. Jay was just a complication. A tempting complication, but no more than that. Like the mystery ingredient she had to incorporate into her dish to meet the challenge the judges had set.

She left her plate as quietly as she could and hurried off to bed. She might have seen Jay having sex with someone else, but in her dreams she was the object of his desire.

When day dawned, Penny still felt hot from the memories of her dream-sex with Jay. She headed straight for the shower to cool off. The cold water was lukewarm, like it always was in the Kimberley, so it wasn't the cold shower she expected, but it was pleasant enough to linger.

Penny reached to turn off the taps when a scream sounded from the next cubicle.

"Oh my God, it's cold! Is there no hot water?" Maia exclaimed.

Penny rubbed herself briskly with a towel. "You get used to it," she called back.

"Not bloody likely," Maia returned. "But better a cold shower than none. Jay's picking someone to take on a date today, Paige said, so we have to look our best."

For the cameras, not Jay, Penny added silently, pulling on her shirt before flinging the door open. She almost hit Daphne.

"Finally!" the other girl huffed, darting into the shower stall. She slammed the door behind her.

Penny heard Daphne's cold water scream from the other end of camp, and from Jay's disgusted expression she judged that he'd heard it, too. She grinned. Daphne might have slept with Jay last night, but she didn't stand a chance with him in the long run.

TWENTY-THREE

"Now, you have to choose one of the girls for a date today," Paige told Jason.

He nodded, his mouth full of cereal.

"We've booked a seaplane with one of the local tour companies, which will take you out to Horizontal Falls. You'll fly over the falls, then land on the water and transfer to a floating dock where – "

"Daphne," Jason mumbled through cornflakes.

" – where you'll enjoy a lunch of fresh-caught fish. You'll get to feed the pet fish, too, before a jet boat ride through the falls to – "

Jason swallowed. "Whatever. Sounds awesome. I'm taking Daphne."

Paige's jaw dropped. "Really? I thought you didn't like her much last night."

Jason shrugged. "You said I have to do a date with each

of them, right? May as well make her first." Because the moment Paige asked him to eliminate one of them, she was gone. The sooner the better. He'd caught her in the kitchen with the tour guide bloke who managed the camp. What was his name? Luke? And not just in the kitchen – going at it hammer and tongs on the bench. Jason didn't think they'd seen him, seeing as the place had been lit by a single solar light, and they were very busy.

At the time, he'd been more surprised than anything, but as the evening progressed, irritation had replaced surprise. Weren't these girls here to try and seduce him, not some cranky tour guide? Not that Jason begrudged him the girl – she'd shown him very clearly that she was the last girl he wanted out of this lot. Tantrums were for two-year-olds, not women he wanted in his life. Two-year-olds were at least three years away, if not more. He wasn't ready to be a father yet. Fuck, it's not like he even had a woman he liked enough to want her to be the mother of his child.

"All right," Paige said haltingly. "I'll get the girls lined up so you can ask her out."

A line-up? He had to assemble them like some sort of army platoon every time he had an announcement to make?

Jason finished his cornflakes and a second cup of coffee before Paige had even half of the girls assembled. Apparently even five minutes of filming required makeup and an extended stint in the bathroom. With six girls and only two small mirrors, that took forever.

He was amused to see that Daphne wasn't last today. That honour went to Lorelei, who finally emerged from the bathroom in a pair of teetering heels, which she then minced along the track with while they waited. Jason had to hand it to her, though – she didn't trip once. That took some skill.

Paige made the girls stand on the edge of the veranda, with the Sound as their stunning backdrop.

The cameraman signalled for them to start.

Jason hated this bit, but Paige had insisted. "Penelope, you made the most delicious meal last night. Calais, you kept me company while everyone else was preparing dinner. Maia and Melissa, you put together that awesome salad. Lorelei, you stoked the fire so it didn't go out. And Daphne, you worked so hard last night, bent over that bench, getting all wet as you did the dishes." He grinned, catching her blush.

One of the other girls made a disgusted sound. He scanned their faces and found the culprit: Penelope. Her expression said she'd caught his innuendo. She probably knew what Daphne had done last night, too.

"But I can only take one of you on a date today, so I choose…." Jason waited for the cameraman to film each of the girl's anxious faces before he got the signal to continue. "Daphne."

Five jaws dropped open with shock, while Daphne sported a coquettish smile.

"Daphne, would you like to spend the day at Horizontal Falls with me?" Jason asked.

"Why, I'd love to," she said, fluttering her eyelashes.

Fuck. Did girls actually do that any more? Or just this crazy one? Jason shook his head. "Great. Let's get going. I got a seaplane on the airstrip, waiting for us."

Daphne threw herself at him in a limpet-like hug. "Oh, oh, oh! I've never seen a seaplane before!"

Jason gritted his teeth. This was going to be a long day.

TWENTY-FOUR

Penny waited until the camera crew had left before she stormed off. Jay had taken the little tramp on the first date! And he'd left them all at the beach camp with nothing to do all day while he took Daphne on an adventure she didn't deserve. Horizontal Falls! For all the time Penny had lived in the Kimberley, she'd never been able to afford to charter a plane or helicopter to visit the natural wonder that was the falls. And it went to ditsy Daphne.

God, the world was so fucking unfair. She followed the track to the bathroom, then kept going, over the dunes, just wanting to walk until her fury was spent.

"Hey, wait up!" Calais called.

Penny didn't want to, but she had to admit Calais had a right to be just as pissed off as Penny was. So Penny stopped, waiting for the puffing girl to catch up.

"Are you going to see the graveyard, too?" Calais asked

when she reached Penny.

Graveyard? "Is that where the track goes?"

"That's what Bec said. It's quite a hike. Some of the graves are more than a century old, from when pearl diving first started out in Western Australia, and the divers had a camp here. She said the other divers built a sort of shrine out of bottles for them." Calais grinned. "We had something like that at my family's farm. No rubbish pick up out there, you see, so my great grandfather started paving the back garden with empty bottles. There's hundreds of them now, and Dad's scared to dig anything up in case he finds more. I think Great Grandpa was a huge drinker."

Calais prattled on and Penny half-listened long enough for her fury to ebb a little. Or maybe it was the hard work of walking up and down endless sand dunes, looking for the mysterious graves. They didn't find them, though they did find a wild beehive in a dead, twisted tree, but finally it was close to lunchtime, so they returned to camp in search of something to eat.

As she bit viciously into her sandwich, Penny hoped Daphne was having as miserable a day as she was. Jay, too.

TWENTY-FIVE

Jason insisted on taking the co-pilot's seat, despite the insistence of both cameramen that he had to sit in the cabin with the rest of them. The plane was too small for him to miss Daphne's squeals of delight at everything from the headsets to the seatbelts to the map in her seat pocket.

After take-off, the squeals were louder and almost constant, but Jason didn't mind them as much. For one thing, the view out the windows was enough to excite him, and the sound of the plane's engines drowned out most of the noise, anyway. He'd heard all the commentary before when he flew to the falls with Gaia, of course, but this time would be different. He got to take a boat through the falls, which he was looking forward to. And he'd heard the saltwater barramundi they served for lunch was some of the best in the world. If that was true, he had to get some supplied to the resort. Romance Island had a reputation for having the best, and Xan would be scandalised to think they were being outdone by a floating barge somewhere else in the Buccaneer Archipelago.

Jason braced himself for a rough landing, but the seaplane skimmed across the surface so smoothly he wanted to applaud the pilot. He wondered if he had the money to get a dedicated seaplane for the resort. Something else to talk to Xan about. Right after he investigated learning to fly one. After all, wasn't John Travolta a pilot? If he'd found time in his busy career to learn to fly, Jason definitely could. Right after he'd dealt with this wife business.

The cameramen climbed out first, insisting that Jason had to help Daphne out of the plane like a proper gentleman. Feeling like a fool, Jason offered her his hand as she hopped onto the floating deck. Daphne wobbled anyway, forcing him to catch her before she fell over. More eyelash fluttering accompanied her profuse thanks, and Jason wondered if the whole thing had been staged. By her or the TV crew? Not that it mattered, really. He set her firmly on her feet and set off to explore what he had to admit was a lot more than just a barge. A network of several multi-level floating platforms, helipads and landing areas for seaplanes, all attached to a luxury yacht, made up the installation. A splash caught his attention and he noticed the massive sea-cage attached to the barges, teeming with huge fish. Lunch, he realised.

The captain and crew assembled on the yacht's deck, lined up much like the girls had this morning. The captain stepped forward, eyeing the cameras. "Welcome aboard the Falls Floating Palace. As you can see, you're our only guests today, as we show you our world-class restaurant, with a view to one of the world's natural wonders. After your lunch, I will personally take you through the only horizontal waterfalls in the world, so you can touch the water for yourself and feel the power of the current."

Jason knew the spiel was more for the viewers at home than himself or Daphne, but she stood rapt at the captain's words. He might not like the girl much, but she was a way better travel companion than Gaia. At least this girl got excited by nature. Maybe the date wouldn't be so bad after all.

Two hours later, he admitted defeat. Daphne had taken every opportunity she could find to bend over things, presenting her backside to him. After a couple glasses of wine, she'd started dropping hints about how she liked to be spanked. Jason had nearly choked on his beer. Shades of Gaia!

He enjoyed the jet boat ride through the falls, whooping loud enough to drown out any noises Daphne made. He knew the camera guys were filming every moment, but that didn't stop him. He didn't care if the world knew he loved thrill rides like this. It was hardly out of character for a rock star. Not like reading romance books.

Jason sighed and stared out of the window. What would the hundreds of romance heroes he'd read about do when faced with Daphne? Probably sweep her off her feet and ravish her, like she evidently wanted. He couldn't summon the enthusiasm to want to, though. Maybe there was something wrong with him. He just wasn't cut out for this hero shit.

TWENTY-SIX

"Oh, that man is hung!" Daphne moaned for what Penny was certain was the dozenth time. "And he wanted me every moment of the day. Couldn't get enough of me. I'll be so sore tomorrow, but, oh! He's so worth it."

Jay and the camera crew had been called urgently back to civilisation, leaving six hopeful brides, two camp managers and a truckload of curiosity in their wake. Curiosity Daphne was only too happy to satisfy with every gory detail.

To hear her tell it, Jay must have been using a supply of Viagra to make it through the day. He'd seduced her on the seaplane, done her on the deck, then fucked her at the Falls four times before doing it doggy-style all the way home. And all with the biggest, hardest dick Daphne had ever seen or felt.

Penny wanted to call bullshit, but she'd seen them at it

last night, and she definitely knew about Jay's reputation. Resignedly, she admitted to herself that Daphne might be telling the truth.

That meant she had to garner attention some other way than sleeping with him. So Penny claimed the kitchen as her territory, cooking every meal and making sure everything was as perfect as it could be, on the off chance that the camera crew returned with Jay in tow.

For two days she slaved, chopping vegetables with a ferocity only matched by her bitterness at Daphne. She wished it was the girl's fingers under her blade and not harmless carrots, but Daphne didn't come near the kitchen. She seemed to think doing the dishes once meant her drudgery was done, especially now she was Jay's favourite girl.

On the third day, Penny had just finished setting up the trestle table for lunch when a boat roared into view, carrying several passengers. She hoped it held supplies, too, as they were getting low on food.

Paige was the first one ashore, carrying her shoes while she walked barefoot through the sand. "Line up! It's elimination day!" she hollered.

Penny prayed that she wouldn't be the one to go. Not that she had the faintest idea who would, though. Jay barely knew any of them. The only one he'd spent much time with was Daphne, and it didn't sound like there'd been much conversation on that date.

It took time to assemble the other girls, who all wanted to redo their hair. Penny didn't need to — she always made sure her appearance was perfect before she entered the kitchen, just in case this was the time she'd be filmed.

Plenty of time for the boatload of supplies to be brought ashore. Ice for the cooler boxes and food enough to last them a week. Less, if Jay and the camera crew stayed, as she hoped.

Wanting to keep her hands busy, Penny grabbed a lettuce before it disappeared into the ice, so she could add it to the selection of sandwich fillings she'd prepared for lunch. She wondered if she should start setting it out now, or wait until after the line-up. Ice clawed at her heart. What if she was the one Jay chose to send home?

"Where's Penelope?" Paige shouted.

Penny stuck her head out the kitchen door. "Here." She shuffled across the veranda to join the other nervous girls. The only one who didn't look scared was Daphne. She looked like the cat who'd gorged herself on canary cream pie as she blew Jay a kiss.

Jay didn't seem to notice. He was busy staring out over the water toward the line of black buoys that marked where the oyster cages floated.

"Right, Jay, you're up," Paige said. One cameraman filmed Jay walking up the beach toward them, while the other kept his lens on the girls.

Jay wouldn't look at any of them. Penny's heart turned colder still.

"Wait!" Paige insisted. "Brides-to-be, you're all Jay's favourites to be his bride. But now, he has to choose to send one of you home. Whoever he sends home won't get to be his wife, and the whole world will know he didn't choose you. Now, I want you to think about how you'll tell your family and friends that you weren't good enough to be a rock god's wife."

Oh God. Penny swallowed, wishing the woman would shut up. As if she wasn't worried enough about this.

She couldn't go home now, and tell her family that, yet again, she'd failed. So Penny prayed for a miracle.

TWENTY-SEVEN

Jason shot Paige a look of irritation. She wasn't making it easy for him. He didn't like making women feel bad about themselves. He rarely rejected anyone for precisely that reason. Oh, Gaia had been an exception, with her overweening pride and that acquisitive look in her eye, at least at the beginning. Then her façade had begun to crack and he'd caved in to her, like he did to every woman.

Yet here he was, supposed to reject someone in front of a recording camera.

Not wanting to repeat the same speech as he had when he'd invited Daphne on a date, he kept it simple this time. "You're all amazing women, and it's been awesome to meet you. But I have to send someone home, and it's a hard decision for me. One I must make." His gaze swept the row of waiting women, meeting every pair of worried eyes before he settled on Daphne, as he knew he had to.

"Daphne, it's time to go home."

Jason wasn't sure which girl was more shocked – Daphne or the others. She recovered first, though. She let out a shriek and marched across the deck toward him.

Jason knew a harpy when he saw one, and this girl was out for blood. His blood. He backed away across the sand, his bare feet carrying him out of her reach, because the girl's heels sank deep into the sand the moment she set foot on it. She pitched forward, but this time no one moved to catch her. This only enraged her further, as she clawed her way along the sand to where Jason stood.

Someone snapped their fingers and two bulky security men hauled the screaming girl to her feet. They dragged her to a waiting four-wheel-drive, bookending her into the back seat, before the car drove off. The sound of her screeching faded away into the dunes.

One of the cameramen had accompanied Daphne, but the other lowered his lens and laughed. "Good thing you had security on hand, or Mr Felix would've copped it. I remember in Season Six, there was this one girl who trashed the farmer's house when she was evicted. Slashed his sofas and everything. And in Five, there was a catfight between two of the girls after an eviction. Lots of hair-pulling and slapping, but not much damage. But that's the first one who really went for the kill."

Paige just shook her head, looking grim.

"I need a beer after that," Jason announced. "Who else wants one?"

The drinks esky was duly brought from the boat, brim-full of beer from the local brewery.

He cracked one open and drank deeply.

"It's barely lunchtime," Paige said disapprovingly.

Jason glanced at his wristband. He'd gotten so used to his resort ID tag that now he didn't take it off at all. After all, it was a GPS and watch, too. "It's three minutes after noon. Definitely drinking time. Lunchtime, too."

"If someone will give me a hand, I'll have lunch on the table in the next few minutes. Everything's ready to go," one of the girls piped up. What was her name? Penelope, that was it.

Jason grinned at her. "Thanks, Penelope. That sounds awesome. I'll give you two hands, if you like."

There was a rush for the kitchen as everyone pitched in to help set out what turned out to be sandwich ingredients, but Jason didn't care. Anything tasted good if it covered the bile that had risen up in his throat when that girl had attacked him. Good riddance. He didn't want a crazy woman who'd try to kill him if he irritated her. No, one homicidal bride was enough for one lifetime.

As Jason munched his sandwich, he tried to decide who he should date next. Penelope, the catering queen? Calais-not-called-after-the-car? Both seemed to have recovered from their shock and were taking their turn at kitchen duty. Lorelei was reapplying lip gloss while Melissa had settled down to read a book. Jason peered at her ereader, hoping it was one he'd read, but he couldn't see the cover at all. Stupid ereaders. Not his style.

The sound of a door slamming drew his eye to the ablutions block at the top of the dune. Maia staggered out of the bathroom, wiping her mouth with the back of her hand, like she'd just been sick. She wearily made her way back to the fire pit that had become their outdoor dining room, refusing all offers of food and drink, even from Paige. Jason waited until Paige returned to the veranda before he asked, "Is she sick? Gastro?"

Paige shook her head. "She said it was just shock at the violence. She'd never seen anyone behave like that, she said."

Jason wished he hadn't. Screaming fans were a normal part of life as a rock star, though usually they screamed for joy.

After lunch, Jason insisted that they all go for a walk on the beach before he let Paige line them up again to await his invitation for the next date.

He couldn't put it off forever, though. Sighing, he surveyed the remaining five girls. They all seemed sane enough. Maia still looked pale, though.

Paige announced what she'd planned for the next date. Nothing special, really. Just dinner and a movie in town, then a night in one of the expensive hotels before returning to Camp Romance.

Watching their faces carefully, Jason made his decision. "Maia, will you come to the movies with me?"

Maia flashed a nervous smile. "Okay."

Her hand was clammy as she took Jason's, but his smile didn't falter as he led her to the jet boat for the first leg of the trip into Broome.

Yes, he had made the right choice this time.

TWENTY-EIGHT

Paige had picked the restaurant, which was a good thing, seeing as Jason usually ended up at the brewery. While the brewery did good food and beer, it held too many memories for him to want to take another girl there just yet. They didn't even get to place an order – Paige had fixed everything in advance, so they got some sort of degustation menu.

"Disgustation?" Jason had quipped when the waiter told him. "Is that where you serve up every strange delicacy you can think of, give us plenty of alcohol to wash it down with, and hope we don't bring it all back up again?"

He couldn't stifle his grin when both Maia and the waiter arced up in defence of the restaurant's premium offering. He'd done plenty of these sorts of meals back on the east coast, especially big charity events the band had been invited to. He hadn't exactly developed a taste for wine, but he could admit that it went well with some foods.

"All right, all right, I'll do it," he said finally when they'd paused for breath. "Just as long as I'm not eating snails. Last time there was way too much garlic on them."

Maia closed her mouth with a snap.

The first course was pearl meat, apparently, served with a slightly fizzy white wine. Jason had visions of having to crunch through pearls, so he was pleasantly surprised to find a slice of oyster on his plate, carefully arranged on a polished pearl shell. The cameraman fixated on it, wanting to film their meal for nearly a minute before he let them eat.

Jason had to admit the pearl meat wasn't bad. Better than snails, anyway. The next course appeared to be a salad with...

"Crocodile," said the waiter proudly.

"It looks like crabmeat," Jason said, forking a bite into his mouth. It didn't taste like crab. It was chewier, too.

More wine washed it down, though, and he asked Maia if she liked it.

She hadn't touched her salad. "Aren't crocodiles endangered?" she whispered.

The waiter heard anyway. "Wild ones are protected, but we get all our meat from a crocodile farm, where they're bred for the luxury leather market, and their meat, of course."

Maia gulped down her entire glass of wine, not touching her plate until the waiter mercifully took it away and replaced it with the next course, some other local product that Jason didn't quite catch. It seemed to satisfy Maia, though, so he figured it was edible.

By about the fifth course, she'd thawed enough to

manage a conversation about her life outside of Camp Romance. Jason learned that she was an accountant, like his sister, and she sounded just as stressed. They just finished dealing with month end accounts when the next set arrived, in an endless cycle of too much work with never enough time, especially as no small business owner seemed capable of filling out the electronic forms correctly, which took dozens of phone calls to clarify. He was pretty sure he'd heard Jo swear about the same things.

The waiter set fire to their dessert, to the cameraman's fascination, before the alcohol burned out and they were allowed to eat the caramelised mounds.

Maia seemed to have talked herself out, so they ate in silence.

Jason cursed inwardly. This was why he didn't date. He sucked at small talk, and all the things he was supposed to do to seduce a woman. Normally his rock star reputation was enough to clinch the deal, but Maia wasn't one of his fans. Like all the girls, she'd submitted her profile without knowing who he was. He regretted that now. It had seemed such a good idea at the time, letting each girl get to know him a bit first before they learned who he was, but now it made the whole affair like a lot of hard work.

Paige had told him time and time again that the viewers wanted romance and kisses, to match the show's ratings, and the more kisses, the better. But he didn't do things that way. Not really. Not since Paige herself, and he'd come a long way from the shy, eager musician he'd been back then.

Maia didn't seem any more eager to lock lips than he did, so Jason was relieved when the cameraman lowered his all-seeing eye to remind them that the movie would start soon.

The lens was turned to them for the walk to the cinema. Jason offered Maia his arm and she curled her fingers into the crook of his elbow. They were forced to wait outside while the cameraman filmed them standing in front of the century-old Sun Cinemas.

Inside…well, that was the funny part, really. The cinema was actually outside again, in the open air. Cloth hammocks slung between parallel poles made up the seats, row after row of them. Jason vaguely remembered something similar at Rottnest, when he'd visited as a kid in the school holidays and they'd turned the old hall into a movie theatre. That was different, though. Sun Cinemas was like a drive-in, without the cars.

Jason and Maia were ushered to the seats in the front row, with several rows cordoned off behind them. It was a weeknight, so the place was pretty empty anyway, but the back three rows were full. Jason grinned. Being a back-seat bogan was more his style, too, but he had to toe the line tonight. If he so much as touched Maia, Paige wanted it captured clearly on film.

Someone had provided them with popcorn and drinks, but no matter how seductively that buttery smell tempted his nostrils, he didn't think he could eat a single bite of the fluffy, yellow kernels. He offered the box to Maia, who shook her head. She'd eaten her fill of dinner, too.

The big, white screen at the front glowed into life, with an ad for some local business.

Something skittered across the screen and Maia jumped. "What was that? A snake?"

More skittering. Jason squinted at the tiny shapes. "Nah.

Just lizards, I think. Geckos, the ones with sticky toes. They climb all over the ceilings at the resort. Like frogs, really. We can't seem to get rid of them. I guess they want to see the movie, too."

"What movie are we seeing?" Maia asked.

Jason shrugged. "I didn't ask. I didn't pick it."

Maia shivered. "I hope it's not scary. Not after today."

Jason slipped a comforting arm around her shoulder. This he knew how to do. "Tell you what. If they screen anything even slightly scary, I'll walk out with you. We can go get a hotel room, order drinks from room service, and watch pay-per-view cartoons until you've had your fill."

Maia nodded. "Deal."

They didn't have a deal, though, as the opening sequence of a romantic comedy flashed up on the screen.

They both shrugged and settled into their sling seats.

Half an hour into the movie, the roar of a jet engine drowned out the sound. Half-lying in the hammock chair, Jason swore as the belly of a plane appeared low overhead, so close it looked like it might hit the screen. It didn't, though – there was plenty of clearance between it and the screen as the plane commenced its ascent to cruising altitude.

As the sound of Qantas' movie crasher died away, Jason became aware of laughter from the back rows. The locals were used to this, it seemed, and they took in the tourists' panic as part of the night's performance.

"I thought it was going to crash, too," Maia whispered, releasing her hold on Jason's hand.

His fingers tingled as circulation returned. "Always an adventure in the Kimberley," he drawled for the camera, before settling in to watch the rest of the movie.

TWENTY-NINE

Jason towelled off his hair in the hotel bathroom, then pulled on his shorts. It was too hot to sleep in any more than that, even with the ever-present air conditioning. He reached for the doorknob, but voices on the other side of the door stopped him. No, just one raised voice – Maia, talking to someone on the phone, he decided.

He knew all about the studio's no-communication rules during filming, so he didn't feel guilty at all for listening in. If he heard what she said, he could decide whether to report the conversation to Paige or not. After all, she could just be ordering room service.

"No, let me talk to him," Maia said. A pause, followed by, "Hello, sweetheart."

Not room service. Jason pressed his ear to the door.

"Mmm-hmm," "Ye-es…" "Well…" and a couple more instances of "Mmm-hmm" punctuated the silence, until

Maia said, "You know you shouldn't watch those movies with Grandpa, because they always give you nightmares."

More silence.

"Then don't watch them. Or tell Grandpa to wait until you're asleep before he watches them. You have plenty of movies and shows on your iPad. Ones that do let you sleep at night. Okay. I'll call back when I can, but I don't know when that will be. Yes, I'll be home as soon as I can, but it might be weeks. I really don't know. Put Grandpa back on, please." A pause. "I love you, too, sweetheart."

Jason listened in fascination as Maia proceeded to deliver a lecture to her dad about what movies her eight-year-old son could watch and why Hannibal Lecter, Freddy Krueger and Jason Voorhees were not appropriate role models for someone Herman's age.

Fuck. He hadn't watched those movies in years. Now he wanted to. Not near Maia, though. She sounded like she hated the entire horror genre. Pity.

Jason made a big show of rattling the doorknob as he unlocked it, so Maia would have a chance to finish her phone call before he wandered in to the living area of their shared apartment. Suite. Whatever it was.

Maia had her back to him, but she evidently knew he was there. "You heard all that, didn't you?"

Jason nodded, then realised she couldn't see him. "Yes."

"You have to tell the people from the TV show about it, don't you?"

"Not if I don't want to."

She spun around and stared at him. "What?"

Jason shrugged. "If it's not captured on camera, as far as they're concerned, it didn't happen. It's not like you're telling show secrets to your family. Are you?"

Maia shook her head slowly. "Of course not. What's to tell, anyway? My son has nightmares enough without hearing about what happened today. He's always had a vivid imagination and Dad's horror movie marathon will give him sleepless nights for months now. He still can't watch that Disney movie with Princess Tiana because the voodoo villain gave him nightmares." Tears spilled down her cheeks. "I'm a bad mother coming up here for so long. I'm all he's got after his dad left. I shouldn't have left him…"

He was getting good at this sympathy thing. Jason moved in for a hug, letting her cry on his chest for as long as she needed. He could have another shower, after all – there was no shortage of hot water at this hotel.

Maia gave a giant sniffle and pulled away from him, backing up a few steps. "Mr Felix, I've had the best night out in years with you tonight, even with lizards, crocodiles and that 747. I'm grateful to you for everything tonight. But I'm not Daphne or Lorelei or one of your fangirls. I…I haven't been with a man since…since…and I don't think…" She waved at his groin.

Jason glanced down. Huh. Hugging her had given him the beginnings of a hard-on, which his shorts didn't hide in the slightest. He tried to think unsexy thoughts. Freddy Krueger's face, for a start. Fuck, that did it. Flaccid as a dead fish.

He cleared his throat. "Paige booked us an apartment, not me. We're sharing because it's easier for the film crew to set up in the living area instead of a normal sized hotel room. There's two bedrooms. We can flip a coin for the bigger bed, if you like, or you can just have it." For the first time, he cursed his rock star reputation. "I've slept with plenty of women, Maia, but they all approached me and asked me for it. I might be a rock star, but I'm a gentleman, I swear. If you want me to get another room on the other side of the hotel, I'll do it."

She stared at him for a long time. Not just his body, but his face, too. Finally, she said, "No, stay here. My tent's closer to your cabin in the camp than the bedrooms are here. Just as long as you don't expect me to…put out…on a first date."

Jason laughed. "And I usually put out without expecting a date. Tonight was different. Normal in a way I never thought I'd get to be again. Thank you." He followed Maia's gaze down his body. "If you change your mind, you only have to ask."

He hadn't made that offer to Daphne, but Maia was different. More down-to-earth. More normal, and fuck knew he needed more normal in his life. Even if it came with an eight-year-old son.

Maia blushed. "I won't. But I wish…" She raised her phone. "Would you let me take a picture? I know I'll regret my decision, but it's the right thing to do. One day I'm going to wish I'd said yes, and if I have a picture to remind me, the fantasy might feel a little more real."

Jason grinned and struck a pose. Several, actually, while Maia blushed and laughed and snapped pictures.

After a few minutes, she remembered herself and put the phone down on the table. "Thank you," she whispered.

"Tell me something," he said. When he had her attention, he continued, "Do you expect a kiss on a first date?"

Maia smiled sadly. "I don't expect anything any more. But if a date goes well, and I like the man, I don't mind a kiss goodnight." Yearning filled her eyes.

Jason wouldn't deny her. He stepped forward, then took another step, until she was within arm's reach again. He lifted a hand to cup her face, caressing her cheek with his thumb. "Good night, Maia."

She closed her eyes and swayed closer, leaning in so her face was millimetres from his.

Jason took a deep breath, then pressed his lips to hers. Soft and pliant, parted the tiniest bit so he could taste her sweet breath, but not her tongue. A sweet kiss, but a short one.

"Sweet dreams, Maia," he whispered, before heading to his bedroom. He closed the door behind him and leaned his head against the cool timber. Fuck. The first of these girls he could seriously consider…but he couldn't, in conscience, keep her away from her son. Thank fuck the cameras hadn't captured any of that.

THIRTY

Penny watched Jay and Maia's return with narrowed eyes, and not just because she was facing the rising sun. Jay helped Maia out of the boat, and she blushed at his touch. That confirmed it, in Penny's eyes. They all knew the pair had spent the night together in town, but Penny was certain they'd spent it in the same bed. Not sleeping.

Was that Jay's plan? He intended to sleep his way through all the girls, and declare the best bonker his bride? That was bullshit. Absolute, complete, utter bullshit. The sun was barely up and her day was already shot to hell.

Savagely, she chopped the bacon into slivers. She'd planned on just dicing it, but now she wanted to turn it into a gourmet omelette that would tantalise Jay's taste buds so thoroughly that he couldn't help but notice her and compliment her cooking.

She sliced the onion finer still, wanting the flavour to

infuse her cooking with none of the texture to distract from the fluffy egg. And it would be fluffy. She'd beat it by hand into fucking froth.

"Whatcha cooking?"

Penny looked up in surprise to find Jay in the kitchen with her, and no Maia. "Breakfast."

Jay jerked his chin at the cutting board. "Looks like more than the toast and cereal I had on my first morning here. Is it a secret recipe?"

Penny twisted her hands together. "Not really. Sort of. I'm just making omelettes, but you have to get the balance right between all the flavours and textures or it's too much. I have onion, bacon, eggs, milk…but what I really want is some freshly grated mozzarella. It gives that cheese taste to it, without overwhelming, and…" She reddened. Swapping recipes with a rock star? Yeah, right.

Jay didn't seem to mind. "Is there anything I can do to help? I'm not much of a cook. Mostly because I never really bothered, and now it's so much easier to just order something from the resort chef."

"You could fire up the barbeque," she suggested half-heartedly.

"Light stuff on fire? I'm your man." Jay grinned, grabbed a box of matches and headed out to the veranda.

Penny watched him, wondering if he'd really do it or if he'd delegate the task to someone else. No, he really was a do-it-himself man, she realised, as he leaned over to get a closer look at the burners as he turned on the gas and clicked the ignitor.

He had a perfect arse, too, she decided, as her eyes fixed on the back of his dark shorts. Curved like a ripe plum, just begging you to bite through the skin…

Jay coughed. He'd caught her checking him out. "Your barbeque is ready and waiting, madame. Is there anything else I can do?"

Bend over like that a lot more, right where I can see you, Penny thought but didn't say. "You could set out the plates while I cook."

"Consider it done."

True to his word, Jay had everything out on the trestle table by the time the hotplate had reached the right temperature. Penny splashed a few drops of water on it to make sure. When the droplets danced to her satisfaction, she spread butter over the cooking surface, watching it bubble just the right amount before she added small spoonfuls of onion and bacon, evenly spaced across the grill. She sautéed each carefully until the onion turned glassy and the bacon sent out its savoury aroma in a clarion call to the rest of the camp. Next, she poured a perfect circle of the egg mixture so that it engulfed one portion of bacon and onion.

Jay clapped. "Breakfast from a master chef!"

Penny glanced up to see the camera firmly fixed on her and Jay. Finally. She took a deep breath and poured another circle, trying and failing to keep her hands from shaking. The second one was more oval than the first, but the third and fourth were properly round again. She wanted to do more, but it was better to be safe than sorry – the first was already bubbling, waiting to be flipped. With a practiced hand that had mastered hundreds of cruise ship pancakes, she flipped the omelette so that it landed without a wrinkle, back on the grill. The second, football-shaped one was easy, but she botched the third, folding one of the edges. Penny paid particular attention to the fourth, so it was perfect.

"You've got to teach me how to do that," Jay breathed.

An apprentice chef, teach a rock star how to cook? That was wrong on so many levels. But she'd look bad if she refused, especially with the camera rolling. "If you want," she said, reaching for a plate to place the first finished omelette on. She added a spoonful of buttered mushrooms, still warm from the pot she'd heated earlier. With a few flicks of her spatula, she folded the omelette like a filled crepe.

Jay held out the next plate, like a well-trained kitchenhand. No, he had the plates laid out along his arm like a well-trained waiter. When had he learned to…?

"I wasn't always a rock star. Starving musicians have to do something to pay the bills, too. And some restaurants even gave me food to take home, so I didn't have to starve." Jay said this in a low voice that only she could hear, but the cameraman was so close that she couldn't be sure. She'd never be able to tell such a personal story like she didn't care if the show shared it on national television. Especially not one that made her look…like a failure. Not that he was a failure now, of course. He was the epitome of success. A rock god, even.

"Can you show me how to do that? I promise I'll eat whatever mess I make," Jay said.

Penny shook her head to clear it. "I guess." She spooned more bacon and onion onto the grill, explaining every step as she stirred and flipped the piles with her spatula. Pouring the egg mixture was simpler, so she just demonstrated for the first three, before handing the jug to Jay. "You try."

Before she could stop him, he poured a slash of egg across the grill, completely missing the onion, but splashing some on his own foot. "Oops."

Penny laughed, wrapped her hand around his much larger one and guided the jug back to where he should have started. An omelette lake formed, merging with Jay's slash so the whole thing looked like Saturn, rings and all. The first three were ready to flip, so she took care of them, handing her spatula to Jay for his planetary pancake. "Run it under the edges to loosen it, then get the spatula right under the middle. You have to get a bit of loft under it when you flip it so it doesn't – "

Saturn splatted in a messy slag heap on the grill.

" – bunch up like that." Penny snatched the spatula and did her best to repair the damage. No matter what she did, it wasn't going to be pretty. She served up the other three, but Jay's misshapen one wouldn't lie flat, let alone fold around the mushrooms. "Look, I can make you another one. There's plenty of batter."

"Nope. I'm good." Jay grabbed a fork and dug in. "Still tastes great. This has to be the best breakfast anyone's ever made me, Penelope." He pressed his lips to her cheek in a fleeting kiss that was over before she'd realised what he was doing. And then he was gone, striding down the steps to the fire pit.

Penny lifted her fingers to her cheek. Compliments and kisses from Jay Felix. On camera, no less. What a beautiful day it was.

THIRTY-ONE

"Who are you taking on the hovercraft on Saturday?" Paige asked Jason during lunch.

He glanced back at the girls, who were all clustered around the table, making their sandwiches. Who hadn't he spent time with? The sun flashed on a head of coppery hair. "Melissa."

"Good choice for a sunset cruise. I hope you plan to kiss her. The boys told me they have exactly one kiss out of all the hours of footage they've taken. One. And that was when you had egg on your face by the barbeque this morning. I'm not even sure we can use that one. Though if you can't do better, we might have to."

Jason screwed his face up in irritation. "What do you mean, if I can't do better? I picked these girls because I think they might be bride material. I don't give a fuck what you think about them or me. You don't want me and that's

119

fine, but that doesn't mean no one does. I'm a fucking rock star now. I can have any girl I want. And I narrowed it down to those five there. I don't want better. They are exactly the sort of girl I want!"

Paige's eyes widened in panic. "I meant a better kiss. That's all!"

Jason wasn't sure he believed her, but he let it go. "Good. And I think that's between me and Penelope, even if we do it in front of your cameras."

"You'd better," Paige muttered.

THIRTY-TWO

All of them assembled on the beach to watch the hovercraft gliding across the water into the bay. Paige had one cameraman concentrating on the people, while the other filmed the sleek craft. Even Jason had to admit it looked like some sort of alien technology left behind from a science fiction film, the way it defied gravity. He wanted one. No, he needed one. The seaplane could wait. He wanted a hovercraft. It beat jet boats hollow. It'd be the perfect runabout around the islands. He could even take it fishing, letting it float on the surface long enough for fish to gather underneath it for the shade, then dropping a line or two over the side to tempt the fish to the surface for lunch.

Not by himself, though. He wanted someone to share it with. One of these girls, maybe. If any of them liked fishing. What if none of them did?

Jason shook himself. So what if his wife didn't like

fishing? He'd take someone else instead. Some of the guys at the resort would be glad to go. Or the pearl farm. They might even be able to point out some good fishing spots, too.

Feeling satisfied with his solution, Jason watched the hovercraft zoom right up to the beach. Everyone clustered around it, exclaiming over the sheer grace of the thing.

Over the excited babble, Paige piped up, "So, Jay, who's the lucky girl that gets to ride in this baby on a very special sunset cruise tonight?"

Five pairs of eyes turned to him, filled with hope.

For a moment, Jason wanted to rescind his earlier decision and take everyone, but he knew Paige had only catered for two.

"Melissa, will you come with me tonight?" he asked, hand out.

She laid her fingers on his palm. "I'd love to."

THIRTY-THREE

The cabin of the craft was pretty cramped. With Melissa, Jason, a cameraman and the…captain? Pilot? The woman driving the thing, anyway…there wasn't really room for anyone else. Jason found himself squeezed into one corner with Melissa while the cameraman put as much space between them as possible, in order to get them both into the shot.

Melissa shook hands with the driver, who insisted they call her Marama. Melissa introduced herself and Jay to the grinning Maori woman, who winked at Jason. He knew he needed no introduction, especially when he knew all the companies catering for his dates with the girls were sponsoring the show by providing their services for free in exchange for TV exposure. Plus, they got celebrity endorsement from a rock star. Cheap at twice the price.

Not that Jason had really done paid product

endorsements. There'd been plenty of offers, from companies selling everything from musical instruments to alcohol to condoms, but Jason had never needed the money. Now…he was getting up close and personal with every tour company in the region. He should be getting their business cards for Xan. She'd jump at the chance to have things as diverse as hovercrafts and seaplanes bringing day trippers to the resort, in addition to the regular helicopter flights and jet boat rides.

Warm fingers squeezed his arm. Oops. He was supposed to be paying attention to Melissa, not thinking about his hotel manager. Xan was probably glad he was gone – she definitely wouldn't be thinking about him. Melissa, on the other hand, turned shining eyes on him. "Did you hear that? Those are billions of years old." She pointed at a cluster of rust-coloured rocks.

That didn't sound right. "But I thought this planet was only a billion years old. Doesn't that mean the rocks came from outer space?"

Both Melissa and Marama laughed. "Earth's around four billion years old," Melissa corrected. "Those rocks are two. So they were formed when the Earth was half the age it is now. And they're still here. The Kimberley must be one of the oldest landscapes in the world. If rocks could talk…I wonder what they'd say, about all the things they've seen." A wistful look misted over her eyes.

Way to make a man feel insignificant. Rock star outperformed by a rock. "They'd probably complain about the good old days, when there were real animals, like dinosaurs, not wallabies and geckos and shit," Jason said.

"Actually, you might be right," Marama piped up.

"There are some dinosaur footprints fossilised into the rock that'll be visible around the point at low tide, in about an hour or so."

"Ooh, will we get to see them?"

Jason opened his mouth to insist on it. To hell with whatever Paige had planned. If the woman wanted dinosaur footprints, then that's what she'd get. He had to admit, he wanted to see them, too. He'd been obsessed with dinosaurs when he was a kid, watching all the *Jurassic Park* movies so many times he could probably still recite the dialogue word for word. Now those were suitable movies to give a boy nightmares. He should mention them to Maia when he got back to camp.

"Of course," Marama replied easily. "They're a scheduled part of the tour. Your TV producer said they weren't romantic enough, but they're one of our tour highlights, seeing as the footprints aren't accessible any other way. I said we visit the footprints, or we don't do the tour. She finally agreed, but couldn't promise that they'd make it through the final cut. Viewers wanted romance, after all."

Melissa eyed Jason. "We could help you with that." She didn't elaborate, though.

"If you can do that, I'll give you both another free tour whenever you want. Without the chaperone." Marama jerked her thumb at the cameraman. Then she resumed her commentary.

Marama pointed out the features along the coast as they passed them, talking about the tides and the history and the local Aboriginal customs until Jason's head felt stuffed full of more facts than he thought possible.

"Every rock has a story, doesn't it?" he blurted out.

"Of course," Melissa said, and laughed. "Sorry, I'm a geologist. I see sentinels that have stood since the beginning of the world; peaks that have been pushed up by volcanic activity or continental shift so long ago that they've eroded into nothing but hills now; sand that's all that remains from what were probably mountain ranges higher than the Himalayas. Marama talks about a rock that's been a favourite family fishing spot for generations, but even Aboriginal history doesn't touch on the amount of time locked up in the rock itself, before there were any humans, or even fish."

So she was smarter than him. Most men might be intimidated, but Jason wasn't. Rock stars didn't need to compensate for shit. Plus, he'd always found smart women sexy.

They cruised along the coastline until Marama said, "We're coming up on those footprints now. I'll need to set you down on the sand. We'll walk the rest of the way." She twisted something on the control panel and the engine coughed into silence. The hovercraft dropped, its air cushion no longer supporting them.

It was still a softer landing than most jets Jason had flown in.

Marama cracked open the hatch. "Watch out, the sand's pretty soft and there's still a bit of water around. If you don't want to get your shoes wet, better leave them here."

Melissa pulled off her sneakers and socks, lining them up beside the open hatch, but Jason didn't care if his thongs got wet, so he kept his shoes on.

"Ladies first," Jason said, executing a low bow.

"Nah, mate, I'll go first," the cameraman insisted, climbing out quickly. He lifted his camera, backing slowly away from the hovercraft. "I'll tell you when I'm ready to record you getting out. Then the lady can go first."

"I'll never get used to having someone filming my every move," Melissa whispered. "How do you cope with the constant attention?"

Jason wanted to tell her that, no matter what she believed, you did get used to it, and he'd even missed it at times. Was a man still a rock star if he wasn't trending on social media any more?

He summoned a smile. "You just grin and bear it, I guess. And try to forget they're there."

"Ready!" came the cameraman's shout.

"Now, ladies first?" Jason ventured.

"I will," Marama said, leaping nimbly out of the craft. "Yep, not quite ankle deep. Perfect timing."

In the end, Melissa insisted on going last, so Jason splashed down next. He reached up to offer Melissa a hand, but she evidently didn't see it, as she jumped down unaided.

They had to wait for Marama to lead the way, but she was deep in conversation with the cameraman. Eventually, she signalled for them to follow her. Hordes of tiny crabs skittered out of the way as they walked through the damp sand and occasional puddles left behind by the retreating tide.

After about fifteen minutes of wandering, Marama called a halt. "There," she said, pointing.

Melissa darted forward, eager to get a closer look. "C'mon, Jay." Her face lit with a wicked smile. "Don't you like dinosaurs? I thought all little boys loved them."

There was nothing little about him now, but Jason had to admit his enthusiasm for dinosaurs hadn't waned over the years. Maybe he should sponsor a dig somewhere, and hope they named one of their discoveries after him.

In the meantime, though, he wanted to see these fossilised footprints.

He was surprised to find they weren't much bigger than his own foot, if considerably wider. He knew not all dinosaurs had been huge, but he'd still expected them to be a lot larger. How had these footprints survived millions of years to still exist today, when the creatures that had made them were dead and gone? He longed to make a mark that lasted for a decade, let alone a million years.

"C'mon, you stand there, and I'll put my feet here. You've got to think like a dinosaur," Melissa said.

Bemused, Jason did as she commanded.

"Marama said they were made by a predator. A therapod, like T-Rex or a velociraptor. A species only found here in Broome, so they named it after the town. I bet when it roared, all the herbivores turned and ran."

Jason snorted. "So if I roar, you'll turn tail and bolt, too?"

Melissa shook her head. "Haven't you watched *Jurassic Park*, Jay? It's the females that were the most fearsome predators. They tend to be bigger, too. If anyone runs, it'll be you."

"Not likely. Try me." Jason placed his feet in two widely spaced footprints, tucking his arms close to his chest like a T-rex, and let loose a roar. He felt ridiculous and awesome, all at the same time.

Melissa laughed. "I think we've got his attention." She

jerked her head at the cameraman. "On three, we'll both do it again, and then we kiss."

Jason nodded, refreshed by her directness. There'd be no beating about the bush with this girl.

He sucked in a deep breath while she counted, then waited for her to begin her truly pitiful roar before drowning her out with his own. By the time he ran out of breath, she was laughing helplessly.

"You win," Melissa gasped, leaning forward.

Jason leaned forward, too, struggling to keep his feet in the footprints until their lips met, but somehow he managed it. They kept their lips pressed together for a few seconds, in an incredibly chaste kiss, before Melissa straightened again, out of reach.

"Now, let's hope that's enough for him to leave us alone for the rest of the evening," Melissa said in a low voice. "And that's the awkward first kiss over with, so if we want another one later, it won't feel quite as weird."

Jason nodded. It sounded logical enough to him. Hardly romantic, and more than a little cold and calculating, but logical. A lot like their kiss had been. No igniting spark, but that could come later. Couldn't it?

On the walk back to the hovercraft, Jason brought up the rear, plagued by the wealth of knowledge he'd picked up in the resort library. From its romance books, particularly, where first kisses were accompanied by sparks and lightning, body parts melting and clenching, as two destined souls connected. He hadn't felt sparks. He wanted fucking electricity, damn it.

It was because of the kiss, not Melissa herself, Jason consoled himself. They'd barely touched lips, let alone kissed each other properly. Next time, there'd be tongues and breath and bodies getting into the mix. A proper kiss. And who knew what could happen after that?

THIRTY-FOUR

Marama landed on a sand cay, still covered in a thin layer of water that reflected the sky better than the mirrors back at Camp Romance. The sun was starting to sink now, and the date was supposed to include a romantic sunset dinner. With water everywhere, it didn't look like a picnic would be particularly practical.

Marama was prepared, though. Out of the hovercraft, she produced a folding table and chairs, then proceeded to set it for two. Food, wine, the works – there was enough for all four of them, Jason thought, and he said as much. Marama just laughed, telling him that there was another basket inside for her and the TV crew.

The cameraman perked up at this. "The sun's not low enough, anyway. I'll break for dinner, and we can go back to filming after."

Melissa kept her eyes on the cameraman until he

disappeared into the hovercraft, when she slumped against the back of her chair. "Finally. What do you say we get to know each other a bit while he's gone? Say all the things we don't want the world to know, so we're left with nothing else to talk about but the weather while we're watching the sunset in front of our audience." She smiled. "Shall I ask the first question?"

"Sure."

"Why did you agree to this reality TV thing? I can't imagine someone like you wanting a wife." Melissa crunched into her dinner.

Jason hesitated, but he knew he needed a ready, rock star reply. "Paige and I go way back. I owed her a favour. She called it in."

Melissa nodded. "Figures. Now, your turn. What do you want to ask me?"

Jason leaned forward. "You said you're a geologist. What's it like? Do you enjoy the work? I mean, it's not all billion-year-old rocks and fossils, is it?"

Melissa sipped her champagne, then set down her glass. "Yeah, I liked it. Right up until the bottom fell out of the iron ore market and the mining companies declared me as redundant as the nipples on Lorelei's silicon breasts." She met his stare. "What? Didn't you know they were fake? It's all in the bounce. Real ones do, and fake ones don't. Find an excuse for her to jump up and down, or run along the beach. Then you'll see it."

Jason made a mental note to do just that. In the interests of science, of course. A rock star might need to know how to spot plastic surgery one day.

"So is that why you decided to join the show?" Jason

asked, trying to keep his thoughts on Melissa's face and not Lorelei's boobs.

Melissa laughed. "Sort of. I mean, six months ago I had a great job, even if it was a bit of a boys' club at work, but I at least felt like one of the guys, you know? Then we all got laid off, and the other guys were finding new jobs, going back to university to get their teaching diplomas and all sorts of things. The night I came home unemployed, my boyfriend – I was living with him at the time – told me not to worry. He'd keep me until I found a new job, he said. I could stay home and take over from the cleaner. He wouldn't even charge me rent, if I did a good job." She drained her wine glass, then poured another, slamming the bottle down into the ice bucket.

From Melissa's simmering fury, Jason didn't figure her for the housewifely type. "So I take it you're definitely single now?"

"Fuck yes. I wasn't putting up with that uppity petroleum engineer a minute longer, lording it over me like it was my poor decisions that crashed the iron ore prices while oil and gas were still going strong. Though it looks like oil prices have dropped now, too. I moved back in with my family, and this seemed like…I don't know, an opportunity. For something new. Maybe even someone new." She raised her glass to him, then drank.

Jason reached for his beer. "Yeah. Maybe."

Melissa set her cutlery on her plate and dabbed her lips with her napkin. "My turn. What's the worst part of the show for you so far?"

"You mean aside from the eliminations?"

Melissa's smile died. "Yeah, that. You looked as shocked

as the rest of us. I guess you aren't used to women trying to kill you."

Jason laughed. "No, I'm used to them wanting to do other things to me."

Melissa lowered her voice. "You know, you're not what I thought you'd be, with your reputation and all. I expected you to be an arrogant arsehole who'd make my ex look like a saint. Instead, you're…kind of nice. I might even buy your next album instead of torrenting it next time."

Jason suppressed a groan. She was one of those people, who thought her work should be paid but all art should be free, with no thought for the hardworking artists who deserved to make a living from their labours, too. Next thing she'd tell him she downloaded pirated books for her ereader, when those took even longer to produce than one of his albums. Months' worth of work, not just weeks.

There was no sound except the waves in the distance as they dug into their dessert.

The hovercraft creaked as the cameraman emerged. "That sunset looks about perfect. You two ready for more filming?"

Saved by the bloke, Jason thought with considerable relief. "Sure. It looks real romantic."

THIRTY-FIVE

The camp was pitch dark by the time Jason and Melissa returned. The fire had burned down to embers, and it looked like all the other girls had gone to bed.

"You know the one thing I miss, living out here?" Melissa whispered.

"Hot showers, a phone, internet access and having a fridge?" Jason suggested, wondering which one she'd pick. She'd told plenty of stories about her geology fieldwork on the trip back, so he knew she was no stranger to camping.

"It's having decent lights at night." She pointed at the dim solar lights lining the track, providing just enough illumination so that you could see where to walk, but not enough to see the tents only a few metres away. "I have one ereader with a light, but the battery's gone flat and I have nowhere to charge it, so I'm stuck with the one that doesn't have a backlight, but it's as bad as a paperback. No light, and I can't read a thing." She nudged him. "What about you?"

"Well, I don't miss the lights," Jason admitted. "Probably because I have reading lights in my cabin. They're solar lights like the rest of the ones here, but these are little concentrated ones clipped to the bedheads. Definitely enough light to read by."

"So what do you miss?" she persisted.

"I wish I'd brought my guitar, to be honest," he said. "I don't play much. Not in months. But lying there, listening to the waves, watching the moonlight on the water, for the first time in ages, I felt like…playing something. And not just playing. Creating something new. It'll probably be terrible. I'd call it *Ode to Camp Romance* and maybe sell it to the studio to use in the credits for the show."

Melissa laughed softly. "Given how big the rest of your band's songs have been, I doubt it'd be bad. You'd probably have a new number one hit on the charts within the week."

"Nah." Jason didn't feel like talking about the band, or why his songs would never hit the charts the way Angel's had. He was supposed to be winning himself a wife to take to Angel's wedding, not writing silly songs. "You know what? If you want to read, I'll still be up for a bit. Probably reading, too. You can come use the light in my cabin for a bit, if you want."

Melissa stopped. "If that's rock star for, 'Come over to my place for sex,' you're barking up the wrong tree, pal. We had one date."

Jason shrugged. "Rock stars don't need to use euphemisms. A dick's a dick, sex is sex and a reading light is a fucking light to read your book by. You want it, the offer's there. You don't, your call." He shuffled into his cabin, leaving Melissa standing in the sand outside.

Shaking his head, he stripped down to his shorts and slid into bed. Not sure what to make of Melissa, he reached under his bed for the books he'd borrowed from the resort library. The top one was a recent release, but it was already tattered from being passed around the female staff. Some sort of adventure romance about a plane crash. As long as it beat the billionaire romances he didn't want to touch any more, it would satisfy him. Jason flipped open the book to the first page.

He hadn't even reached the first sex scene when someone knocked tentatively on his door. "Mmm?" he said.

The door swung open. "Is your offer still open?" Melissa whispered. She'd changed into a pair of pyjamas and the strong smell of mint made Jason think she'd probably brushed her teeth, too.

"I'm using this light, but there's another one on that bed." Jason pointed. Yes, single beds on opposite sides of the room. She could make of that whatever she wanted. "There's linen in that locker if you need it." He went back to his book.

Jason heard her messing around in the locker, clicking on the light and finally settling on the slightly squeaky mattress springs, but he didn't so much as glance up. That was the whole point of reading — you got lost in your own little world, and the real world could go get fucked.

Speaking of fucked…

The mattress squeaked as Melissa shifted from lying on her belly to curled on her side, facing the wall. Her knuckles whitened as her fingers tightened around her ereader.

A really scary bit, Jason decided.

Melissa bit her lip.

The penny dropped. "You're reading a sex scene, aren't you?" he blurted out.

Melissa turned red. "And what if I am?" she challenged.

"Is it a good one?" Jason persisted.

"Maybe."

He gave in. "Can I read it?"

Melissa clutched her ereader to her chest. "I don't think so. I'm reading it right now."

A really hot sex scene, then, and a good one. Jason couldn't resist. "I could read it aloud, if you like. Kind of like sharing, only better. I used to do voiceovers for radio ads before the band made it big. I can do deep and sexy, the way a book's supposed to be read."

Melissa eyed him. "A rock star reading romance?"

Jason slid his own romance novel under his pillow. "I'll give it a go. If I suck at it, you can always tell me to stop."

She considered for a long moment, then extended her ereader across the divide between the two beds. "The scene starts from that page."

Jason skimmed the first few lines. Foreplay. Not his usual way of starting a seduction, but if that's what floated her boat...

He took a deep breath and began to read.

THIRTY-SIX

"Oh my God, Jay, stop!" a feminine voice squealed as Penny left the bathroom.

The voice only grew louder as Penny approached Jay's cabin.

"Please! I can't breathe from – " muffled words Penny couldn't discern " – so hard!"

Jay said something, too low for Penny to hear.

"But that bit with the tongue! I seriously thought I'd explode. Oh my God!" Melissa's words disappeared in a squeal.

Let the best bonker win, Penny fumed, stomping back to her tent. Jay really was sleeping his way through the contestants. He hadn't even asked her on a date yet, let alone invited her to have sex. Did that mean he didn't want her?

Penny's heart froze at the sound of a delighted giggle

from his cabin.
The world just wasn't fair.

140

THIRTY-SEVEN

"Please! I can't breathe from laughing so hard!" Melissa gasped.

Jason dropped his voice lower, drawing out each word as he read the paragraph again, trying in vain to imagine the scene the author had described. He was an expert with his tongue, as hundreds of girls had told him, but even he didn't think that was physically possible. He bit his tongue before mentioning that to Melissa, though. She really seemed to like the book.

"I'm going to sleep," he told her. "You can stay there as long as you like. Reading, sleeping, whatever. I don't mind. Not like I need the other bed."

With the practiced ease of a man who could sleep anywhere, Jason drifted off into dreamland.

When day dawned, he found Melissa fast asleep in the other bed, with her ereader pillowed on her chest.

Jason grabbed some clothes as quietly as he could and headed for the shower without waking her.

THIRTY-EIGHT

Penny whisked the pancake batter within an inch of its life, or she would have if it'd had one, as she watched Jay emerge from his cabin and stumble to the bathroom. A few moments later, Melissa slipped out, too, looking like she'd just woken up. Had she and Jay been at it all night? Penny dug her nails into the whisk handle. At least they'd kept it quiet for most of the time. He'd stopped making her squeal after Penny's bathroom break, or maybe Penny had just slept through it. Thank God for small mercies, whichever it was.

There was nothing worse than listening to someone else have sex with the man you wanted and couldn't have.

Wait, what?

Penny almost dropped the whisk, but caught it in time.

She didn't want Jay. She wanted the world to see her cooking. She should get back to it, Penny told herself. The pancakes wouldn't make themselves.

Penny busied herself, firing up the barbeque and finding a bowl for the syrup, so it could warm on a corner of the grill while she cooked pancakes for everyone. She knew it wasn't her job; the camp managers, Bec and lazy Luke, were supposed to cook, but she was calmer in the kitchen. She didn't want to kill everyone, and the need to rip out some bitch's hair or claw her eyes out…lessened, a little, at least. She could forget about everyone else when she was thinking about food.

The grill was hot enough now. Time to concentrate on turning the thick mixture into perfect, fluffy circles. Penny poured a single pancake, just to test the temperature, peering at it as she flipped it, to make sure she had the timing right for the rest, then slid it onto a plate when she was done. She spooned out a dozen evenly-spaced circles on the hotplate, watching with satisfaction at how well she'd measured out the mix. They'd stack perfectly on a plate, ready to be drizzled with syrup. Not maple syrup, like she wanted, but golden syrup would do. If only they had fresh blueberries…

"That smells incredible. Like cake."

Penny turned and found herself face to face with Jay. He wore nothing but a pair of shorts, his perfectly muscled chest and abs on display for all to stare at. Or just her, right now, seeing as they were alone on the veranda.

"Pancakes," she corrected. "And it's probably just the syrup you can smell." She waved at the bowl.

"I haven't had pancakes in months. This is the last place I expected to get some. I am officially in love."

Penny found herself enfolded in his arms, pressed

against that hard body in a hug as hot as it was unexpected. She stared up at him, letting out a gasp as her body melted like butter at his touch. Unable to say anything, unable to even think, she did what her body was screaming at her to do. Penny kissed him.

Jay's hand moved to the back of her head, his tongue tickling hers as he took the lead in this dance. She couldn't suppress a moan as her lips moulded to his, her tongue tingling as it explored his mouth. She wanted to wrap her legs around his waist and beg him to take her on the table, then and there, wreathed in the scent of vanilla and eggs and sweet, sweet syrup...

"Well, good morning," Paige said.

Penny peeled her hand off Jay's bottom, wondering if his searingly hot kiss had actually caramelised her lips. They felt burned, like he hadn't stopped kissing her at all, instead of stepping away to greet Paige and the ever present camera crew. Who looked like they'd caught the whole thing on film...

Penny ducked her head, trying to hide her red cheeks, as she dealt feverishly with the pancakes before they burned. She didn't want Jay. She wanted...

She needed him. Every perfect inch of him, from top to toe and every bit in between. Her mouth parched at the thought.

"You took your time," Jay said to Paige. "I want to get the next elimination over and done with. This morning, if we can."

Penny's spatula slipped, sending a pancake tumbling to the deck. Elimination? Was that why Jay had kissed her? Was he saying goodbye? Sure, he was in love...with someone else.

Lorelei. Or Maia. Or Melissa. The sluts who'd already opened their legs for him, while Paige had interrupted Penny before she could have Jay. Was that her game? Was Paige setting Penny up to be the bitch, because the real bitches were Jay's favourites, so she had to make them look good?

Did Jay know? Maybe that's why he intended to send Penny home. He was too kind to let her be Paige's bitch for the rest of the show, so he was helping her escape. So much for cooking on national television. Paige would hide all the good stuff, and only show the bad, as she tried to make the whole country hate her,

Penny blinked back tears, forcing herself to focus on spooning out the next batch of pancakes. The perfect circles wavered in her vision. This whole mess had been a horrible mistake.

THIRTY-NINE

Jason munched his way through a stack of sublime pancakes while the girls took turns in the bathrooms. They wanted to look good for the line-up. For the first time, he wondered if they did it for him or for the cameras. Were they trying to catch the eye of some talent scout who saw them on their screen, or did they honestly think a perfectly lipsticked pout beneath mascara-slicked lashes would change his mind about sending them home?

He shook his head. They evidently had never paid attention to the girls in the band. Both Angel and Jo had worn enough stage makeup to blend in at a KISS concert. Anonymity after the concerts had been easy for them – just wash the muck off and walk out, without a single fan identifying them.

These girls wanted to be noticed. But could they handle the sort of media attention he dealt with every day? All right, he didn't now, but if he ever made a comeback tour, the reporters would be back with a vengeance. He already had Paige's answer: no. No girl could cope, standing beside Jay Felix in the limelight. She'd be buried in a storm of hate.

Now, Melissa might be able to handle it. She'd probably give as good as she got. He figured Lorelei might manage, too, but in a completely different way. Lorelei would smile for the cameras, bat her eyelashes, and completely ignore anything they had to say that wasn't a compliment. She couldn't really be that shallow – no one could – but if the media bought it…

Then there was Calais and Maia and Penelope. Capable women that he really liked. But Penelope's face mirrored her feelings. She couldn't hide anything from the press. Maia had her son to protect, but it was only a matter of time before the media found out about him, and then the speculation would start. If you listened to the media for long enough, you'd believe that half the fatherless bastards in Australia were the fruit of his loins, and a truckload in America, too. Never mind that he'd never failed to return a negative fatherhood test for every baby. And Calais, who had clammed up so much he'd barely managed to get more than ten words out of her since she'd arrived at the camp…

Jason shook his head. He didn't have to worry about the media today, though. The show wouldn't screen on TV for weeks yet, so there wouldn't be any media waiting at the airport for the girl he sent home today.

He scanned today's line-up. Penelope's face showed outright panic. Calais was intent on her shoes, as usual. Lorelei and Melissa both wore confident smiles, and Maia just looked resigned. Time to put them out of their misery.

Jason marched up the veranda steps, babbling for the benefit of the camera about how hard it was to choose one girl out of all his favourites. He hoped Paige chose to cut that bit when it came to editing. When he reached the girls, he halted a couple metres away, so he could see all of their faces. He didn't need to – he knew exactly whose eyes he needed to meet.

"Maia, it's time to go home," he said softly.

Her breath hissed out in an obvious sigh of relief.

Jason took heart. He'd made the right decision. "I know you're needed at home more than you need to be here. I've had an awesome time with you, especially on our date in town the other night, but I can't be selfish. Life isn't all popcorn and pearl meat. There's the odd Friday the 13th tucked in among all the perfect days."

Maia smiled. She understood the oblique reference to her son, even if no one else did. She strode forward and so did the security guards, but Jason signalled for them to stay back. Maia wasn't going to kill him, he was sure of it.

He was right, too. She flung her arms around his neck and kissed his cheek, murmuring, "Thank you," before she trotted off to her tent to collect her things.

"I'll want to do some individual interviews with the girls," Paige said briskly. "Jay, you stay beside the car with Wes. Wes, you make sure you get some good footage of him and Maia saying goodbye, and her driving off. Right, I'll have Melissa up first, and Penelope next. We'll set up on that rock beside the beach, so there's a nice backdrop. Cole, you come with me."

Calais rushed past Jason, as if she was busting to use the bathroom, but Jason was surprised to see tears streaming from her reddened eyes. What had he done to make her cry?

Jay hesitated for just long enough for Paige to disappear from view, before he made up his mind. It was time to get to know the enigmatic Calais. He wanted to see her smile like she had in their speed-dating interview.

FORTY

Feeling like the world's most inept stalker, Jason followed the girl across the sand dunes, slipping and sliding so many times that he lost his thongs twice before she finally came to a halt at the top of a rust-coloured dune that was higher than the rest. From this vantage point, you could see clear out to sea, and even the western edge of the Buccaneer Archipelago. Not quite as far as Romance Island, but Jason didn't need to see his island to know where it lay.

Oblivious to the view, Calais sank to her knees and wept.

Jason was lost. He had no experience with this sort of heartbreak. Oh, unless you counted Angel in the early days after her abduction, but offering her comfort back then would earn you a knife in the goolies just as surely as saying you'd seen her cry.

So he said what any sane bloke would in the situation:

"What did I do to upset you?"

Calais sniffled and peered up at him. "Nothing," she said finally.

Jason squatted on the sand beside her. "So what didn't I do that you think I should have?"

A tiny laugh erupted from Calais. "I don't know."

Jason was all out of inspiration, but he didn't want to leave her here, either. So he sat there in silence, hoping she'd break it.

After maybe ten minutes of staring out over the ocean, Calais said, "It's nothing you did or didn't do. It's this whole situation. I hate being in a…harem. At your beck and call, waiting through the boredom until you make your selection of just one of us for a day or a night, then you bring us back here to await your pleasure, whenever that might be."

Jason tried to wrap his head around her words. "A harem? I don't think of any of you like that. Isn't a harem just for sex and babies, where everyone wears those sexy, see-through pants? And there's eunuchs?" He covered his jewels at the thought.

"There's Luke, the camp manager. He might be a eunuch," Calais offered.

Jason shook his head. "Nope. He did Daphne in the kitchen on the first night."

"No!" she exclaimed.

"Oh, yes. I saw them. I got out of the kitchen real quick, before they saw me."

Calais tapped her chin. "So that's why you sent her home. Did Maia sleep with him, too?"

"I don't know. I don't think so." Jason closed his mouth before he betrayed Maia's secrets. "Just not my type, I guess." And her son needed her.

Calais eyed him. "So it's not just a publicity stunt. Are you really looking for a wife?"

"Maybe," he hedged. "What about you?"

She sighed. "No, I'm not looking for a wife. I didn't even enter. Not really. My brother submitted for me when I wasn't going to. I think he was trying to help, but…today just made it worse, not better."

And that wasn't cryptic at all. "So let me get this straight. You were in some woman's harem before, but your brother pulled you out so that you could learn to like men instead, but I remind you of everything you hate about men, or the unfairness that gay marriage isn't legal in Australia yet?"

Calais laughed properly then. "No, I like guys, or I did. I just…someone very close to me was in a restrictive relationship, where her partner kept her isolated, just like we are here, until she pretty much depended on him for everything. And when he didn't…didn't love her any more, she died. Suicide." Calais pressed her lips together, shaking her head firmly. "So I don't like harems. And I think I realised that today, when we were all lining up, and everyone looked to you for your favour. I wanted to scream that it was wrong and we should all go home."

"But you didn't."

Calais shuddered. "And turn it into a horror scene like when Daphne left? No thanks. I'm not a raving lunatic. So I held together as long as I could, before coming up here to be alone."

Jason nodded. He took that as his cue to head back to camp. He needed to talk to Paige.

FORTY-ONE

"But what about your next date?" Paige hissed. "You have to pick one of them and – "

"I'm going home to the resort," Jason said. "When I come back out here, we'll see." He climbed into the jet boat, nodded to Baz, and ignored Paige as they set off across King Sound.

Jason barely noticed the changing tides as the boat skirted around the whirlpools at the entrance to the Sound, and then they were around the point, skimming between the islands of the archipelago. He needed to think. He needed to talk to someone. A woman, preferably, who didn't have a stake in all this craziness.

His first thought was his sister, Jo. She'd be honest, and she wouldn't hold back, either.

The moment he walked into his villa, he headed straight for the phone. Jo made it halfway through her greeting before Jason asked, "Are reality TV shows degrading?"

Jo didn't hesitate. "God, yes. Degrading to the people in them, and more degrading still to the idiots who watch them. I stopped watching TV almost entirely because of them. It's not reality. It's a warped, distorted view, manipulated by the TV producers and the people that agree to the whole farce."

"Including the dating shows?"

Jo made a noise of disgust, deep in her throat. "Those are even worse. You mean like the rural romance one the resort's hosting? I know it's good for the resort, because Xan gets to show the place off, but I don't know how anyone can sign up for one of those. They'd have to be desperate for love, if they think they can find it in a matter of days with a bunch of complete strangers. Not to mention…it's not one stranger at a time. It's all the girls competing for Desperate-and-Dateless's attention while he seduces all of them. I bet if the show didn't have a PG rating, there'd be mass orgies going on behind the scenes. There probably are, but just not on the bits they show on TV."

She sure did know a lot about them.

"Thanks, Jo." He walked over to the cradle to put the phone back.

"Wait…why are you asking? Are you thinking about…no, Jason. Don't. Just don't. If you – "

Jason set the phone firmly on the charger, ending the call before he had to lie to Jo.

She hadn't answered his question, though. Not really. She'd been so against all such shows that he couldn't bring himself to ask her.

Sighing, Jason strode out to the jetty. He thought better walking the boards, than he did cooped up inside. Something about the sea air, or something. Not that it smelled any different to the air at Camp Romance. Just being alone, maybe…

"I thought I saw you come in."

Or not.

"Had enough of your harem already?"

Again with that word. Jason stared at Xan. "Are harems degrading to women?"

Xan snorted. "Blood hell, yes. They're the ultimate expression of male power. Keeping a bunch of women locked away from the world, existing solely for your pleasure? It's barbaric."

"So I'm a barbarian now?" he tested.

"Only if you've turned them all into sex slaves." Xan blinked. "You haven't, have you? Woven some sort of rock star spell over them, the way you have all the other girls I've seen you with, so they'll agree to share you?"

"Not that I know of." Jason broke into a smile. "You seriously think I'd be capable of that?"

Xan's expression grew unusually blank. "Well, look at the evidence. Phuong, Flavia, Gaia…and all the girls who came before. I guess the only question would be…why haven't you done something like this earlier, if that's what you wanted?"

Jason shook his head slowly. "I never wanted a harem. Not before, and not out of the show. I only wanted one woman, and now… One of the girls today said she felt like a harem girl. That they all were. If she's right, it's wrong, isn't it?"

"Which part?" Xan asked. "The bit where you have multiple girls at the same time, or that the whole sordid story gets filmed for TV?"

"That they have no real choice. No say in how things play out. Who goes on what date. Who spends time with me and when. Who has to go home…I make the decisions. I make them for them. Who gave me all that power? And what if I make the wrong decision? I don't want to fuck this up."

"So let the girls decide."

It sounded like such a brilliant idea…but… "Paige will never go for it," Jason declared. "She said the show has to follow the standard format. The eliminations, the dates, the family dinner, the final decision…"

Xan broke into a wry smile. "There's no format for a dating show with one rock star bachelor. Her format is for a bunch of farmers who all have to follow the same storyline. You've already messed with that just by being you. And you get to see all the footage, which I'm sure no other bachelor from the previous seasons got to see before he made his decisions. Do the girls suspect when you leave on business, you're actually just rushing back here to watch the bits you missed? I think if you tell Paige to do things differently, she'd accommodate you. She's still under your spell a bit, you know."

"No. Not Paige."

Xan shrugged. "Try her and see. After all, without a bachelor, she has no show."

FORTY-TWO

The next morning, Jason was woken by the intercom, informing him he had a visitor. The calm, recorded voice repeated the message as Jason stumbled to the front door. He cursed back, asking it why it couldn't tell him the name of his visitor. All staff and guests wore wristbands, after all. If he opened the door and found a fucking frog…

"Jay, you need to come back. The date, remember?" Paige called through the door.

Not a frog. Not a guest or staff, either, and probably not wearing a wristband if she didn't intend to remain on the island.

Time to see if Xan was right about Paige.

Jason palmed open the door. Desire flamed in Paige's eyes as she took in his nakedness. One point to Xan. "Let the girls decide," he said.

Puzzlement creased Paige's forehead. "What?"

"I'm not going to pick the girls for each date. They should get to pick what they want. Offer them the different dates and let them decide which ones they want to go on with me. If they want to." Calais might not want to, and Penelope… "Give them a choice."

"I can't. Some of the excursions are way better than the others. I mean, there's a helicopter ride, a jet boat ride, a charter flight, a pearl farm tour with a night in the deluxe safari tent…and all of them include romantic dinners at some really spectacular locations. They'll all pick the best one."

Jason shrugged. "So make them compete for it. Whoever comes first, gets to pick first, until they all do. Schedule the dates and that's what we do."

"But the viewers love the bit where the blokes ask. It's romantic," Paige protested.

"I can still ask them out, and if you keep the schedule a surprise, they'll still look surprised when I ask, because they won't know which day," Jason offered.

Paige wavered. "But they're already competing for you. What else do you expect them to do?"

"I don't know. Something more taxing than putting on makeup and the most revealing clothes they own. Make them run sprints, or arrange flowers, or mud wrestle, or play a chess tournament. I don't care. Making good TV is your job. If they want first pick, they'll try harder. If they don't, that's fine. They don't have to go on a date with me if they don't want to. But every time I choose, it's like going into a brothel and picking someone for the night. It doesn't feel right."

Paige eyed him. "You've been into a brothel? YOU?"

Jason squirmed. "Once, all right? A bunch of guys from uni decided to drive out to Kalgoorlie and see the sights. That included the historic brothels."

Paige whistled. "So somewhere in the wilds of Western Australia, there's a working girl who got paid to sleep with the legendary Jay Felix."

"I didn't say that. I said I went into the brothel. I was a starving uni student. I could barely afford more than two beers. An hour with one of those girls? Way beyond my means back then. Nah, I just sat in the bar, nursing my beer, making the girls laugh while they were waiting for work."

Paige still looked puzzled. "You're a strange man, Jay."

He shrugged. "There's only one of me in all the world. Which is why the world loves me, of course. And you know it. So, are we doing this?"

"All right," she said slowly. "But not mud wrestling."

Jason sighed. "All right."

FORTY-THREE

"Right, there's been a change of plan," Paige announced.

Inwardly, Penny groaned. Without Jay there, she figured it meant no date tonight, but Paige had brought ashore a whole bunch of boxes that were piled up in the kitchen, before she'd declared the whole structure off limits for the girls.

Lazy Luke had smirked at that, until Bec nudged him and said he was making dinner tonight.

"We're having a little friendly competition," Paige continued. "Whoever comes first, gets to choose where they go with Jay on their date. Second gets next pick, until all the dates are allocated."

"What do we have to do?" Melissa asked.

She'd already had a date with Jay. She should automatically go last, Penny fumed.

Paige smiled widely. "First, you're going to pick a dozen

– that's twelve – roses from the boxes in the kitchen. Then, you're going to carry them to the top of the ridge, where you'll find four vases. You're to arrange your flowers in one vase, before coming back down to the bathroom block for fresh water. You'll carry the water in those clam shells on the veranda until the vase is full to the level marked on the side. First girl to fill her vase, wins!"

It sounded like a lot of work for the privilege of picking where you went on a date. "What if we don't do it?" Penny asked.

"Then you don't get a date with Jay at all," Paige replied. And be the next girl sent home, she didn't add, but then she didn't have to. They all knew it.

Penny sighed. Flower arranging. Couldn't be that hard, could it?

Paige lined them up, then released them with a, "Ready, set, GO!"

All four of them bolted for the kitchen. Lorelei managed to push Penny out of the way so she could squeeze through the doorway first, but her momentary lead didn't help her. The boxes were taped shut, and Lorelei's acrylic talons were no use. Penny reached automatically for a knife and sliced her way into her box. She counted out the roses – only ten. Another box gave way to her cutting skills and she had a dozen roses in her arms. She sprinted for the door, with Melissa right behind her.

The track to the ridge was wide enough for all four of them to run abreast, so Penny didn't mind so much when Melissa kept pace with her. Reaching the top of the ridge, Penny scanned the sand and scrub for the vases. Someone had placed them in the only cleared spot – grouped around the base of a dead snag that held a wild beehive in its hollow trunk.

The few bees buzzing high over her head didn't seem to care about her, though, so Penny ignored them to head back down the dune for water.

The clam shells were roughly the size of large soup bowls, and they balanced nicely in her hand just like a bowl. Penny grinned, grabbing a stack of them and proceeded to fill them from the tap before placing them along her arms. She managed six before the weight became too much, then strode carefully up the dune. Melissa sprinted past her, looking stunned, but the girl didn't stop.

Penny reached her vase with most of the water still in the shells, so she poured it carefully in. They only filled a quarter of the big vase, which meant three more trips, at least. Penny stacked up her shells and ran back for a refill.

This time, she had to wait in line behind Lorelei and Calais, who hadn't seen her waitressing technique, so they only carried one shell each. Melissa had two, which she filled before taking off at a fast clip.

When Penny's shells were full again, she didn't hurry. Speed wasn't as important as steadiness, so she wouldn't spill…

Lorelei bumped into her on her way down the hill, upsetting all three of the shells on Penny's right arm. Penny cursed, convinced the bitch had done it on purpose. Lorelei just stuck out her tongue and veered off.

Penny poured. Not half full yet. Another three trips still. Down she went.

The next two trips she managed not to spill much, but the water level was still a good inch shy of the fill line, though much higher than anyone else's. One of them barely had an inch in it. One last trip, she promised herself. Then she could choose her date with Jay. That meant she had to stay long enough for that, at least.

Penny was halfway up the dune when she heard Paige's shout ring out behind her. "We have a winner!"

On top of the ridge, Lorelei held her brimming vase aloft, her face split in a triumphant grin.

What? How? It wasn't possible. There was no way Lorelei had carried enough water up that hill to fill a vase more than halfway.

Penny reached her vase, which had somehow tipped over, leaving nothing but a trickle of water at the bottom. Yet the sand was dry, showing no signs of spillage. She glared at Lorelei, knowing what the girl had done. Throwing her shells on the sand, Penny marched up to the lying, cheating bitch and punched her in her perfect nose. Lorelei went down like a sack of potatoes.

Penny was good at mashed potatoes, come to think of it. She reached for the nearest vase, one that still had water in it, and raised it over Lorelei's head.

A piercing scream came from Penny's other side, distracting her.

Melissa's face was ashen as she clutched her arm. "A bee. It stung me."

"Brush it off," Calais advised. "You'll be fine."

"No, I won't," Melissa whispered, swaying. "I'm mortally allergic to bees. I need to get to hospital. Now. Or I'll die."

Penny could kill Lorelei later. Melissa didn't deserve to die yet. Calais and Penny moved to support Melissa, one under each arm, carrying her down the hill. Calais explained breathlessly to Paige while Bec brought out the first aid kit. Someone found some sort of injector, which Bec stabbed into Melissa's leg, while Penny looked away.

Before Penny knew it, Melissa was whisked away in the four-wheel-drive, to meet the Royal Flying Doctor Service plane winging its way to the pearl farm air strip.

It wasn't until after eating a dinner of Luke's specialty – burned barbeque – that Paige came to ask Penny which date she preferred. Penny took one look at the list and picked the helicopter tour to the pearl farm on the other side of the peninsula. They'd arrive by helicopter, have a seafood banquet with champagne and cruise the creek the pearl farm was named for. Now, if she could just negotiate with the chef to be allowed to prepare the food instead of him…

"Lorelei already picked that one," Paige said. "You'll have to pick something else."

"She cheated!" Penny returned hotly. "She had barely any water in hers, while mine was nearly full. She stole mine and cheated!"

"On the footage we have, she won, so she picked first," Paige said evenly. "Unless someone videoed her doing what you said, there's no proof. And as Melissa has now been airlifted to Perth, we can't redo the race, so the result will have to stand. Make your choice, or no date."

"What's left?" Penny asked, fighting to keep her voice calm. Now she wanted to break Paige's nose so she matched Lorelei. But if she did that to the show host, she'd be cast as the bitch for sure.

"A charter flight to some waterfall, or a night in the luxury safari tents at this pearl farm."

"The tent night," Penny said promptly. She wasn't giving anyone else a chance to spend the night with Jay.

"Done," Paige said.

No, they weren't, but Penny could be patient. She'd bide her time, but she'd get her revenge on Lorelei. Maybe even on Paige, too. If she could get Jay to choose her over Calais and Lorelei, then Paige would have to make her look wonderful in every episode.

All she had to do was win the rock star's heart. He'd already kissed her twice, and he'd said he was in love, though he might have been talking about her cooking more than her. Still, he had said love. How hard could it be?

FORTY-FOUR

"So how did the competition go?" Jason asked Paige when she appeared in the conference room that had become the film crew's editing studio. He eyed the hard drive in her hands that held the previous day's footage. He'd finally caught up on everything he'd missed over the last week, and some of the interviews had been eye-openers.

Melissa had admitted she guessed that Maia would be sent home, after watching Maia distance herself from the rest of them, following her date with Jay. Melissa then went on to say that Jay had "hidden depths" that she'd like to explore, and she was looking forward to having the opportunity, because he was just the sort of man she could see her future with.

Jason wasn't sure whether to believe her or not. He'd gotten the impression that she hadn't liked him all that much, but maybe he'd been wrong. After all, there was a big difference between throwing herself at him like the fangirls did and hating his guts. He could hardly compare her to a fangirl.

Lorelei had giggled about how compatible they were, dropping heavy hints about how much sex they'd had and how good it was. This was news to Jason. Unless he'd met her before the show and forgotten – entirely possible, give how many groupies he'd slept with over the years – he'd never so much as kissed the woman, let alone had sex with her.

Penelope and Calais…those two answered the questions, but they hadn't said much. The only thing that stuck in Jason's mind from those two interviews was the one point they'd both made: neither of them knew him well enough to say whether he was marriage material for them.

More time. He needed more time. Watching the videos was one thing, but he needed to spend more time with all of them before he made up his mind. If he had to make a decision now, he'd pick Melissa, but only because he didn't know the other girls as well.

"It's Melissa," Paige said.

Jason realised he hadn't heard a word she'd said up until she mentioned Melissa's name. "What?"

Irritation crossed Paige's face as she evidently came to the same realisation. "I said one of the girls got hurt. She had to be airlifted to hospital in Perth. Melissa."

No. That couldn't be right. "How?" he demanded.

Paige held up the hard disk. "That's what I'm here to see." She plugged in the USB.

Melissa. Gone. "So is she coming back?" Jason asked while they waited for the files to load.

Paige shook her head. "She had a really bad allergic reaction. They're keeping her in for a few days for observation." She summoned a smile. "At least you won't have to worry about doing another elimination this week."

"Yeah, but..." He hadn't intended to send Melissa home. He wanted her to stay. Now, more than ever, he needed to get acquainted with the other girls.

"This is raw footage from the camera at the top of the hill. I was at the bottom, so I didn't see," Paige warned, her hand hovering over the mouse.

Jason nodded. Most of the other stuff he'd seen hadn't been edited, either, or at least he didn't think so. Of course, Paige could have held back some of the footage, if she hadn't wanted him to see it, but he didn't think she'd be that manipulative. At least, the girl he'd known six years ago wouldn't have been. Surely Paige couldn't have changed that much in six years. He knew he hadn't. Well, aside from more time in the gym and all that experience in the bedroom, and wherever else girls had wanted him. And the romance research in the resort library...nah, he hadn't changed. Not really.

The video began to play and Jason listened intently to Paige's shouted instructions to the contestants. "Flower arranging and running sprints?" he asked. "Chess not exciting enough for you?"

Paige hushed him, her eyes on the screen.

The footage faded to black, then cut in to a different scene. The glass vases grouped around the twisted tree looked like some sort of backdrop for a photo shoot. One of those fashion ones with weird clothes no one would wear unless the apocalypse had truly come and they had nothing else. No half-starved models today, though.

The camera panned to the camp at the bottom of the hill, where Paige stood. Two figures raced across the kitchen veranda, each carrying an armload of flowers. The girls pelted up the hill, neck and neck, and Jason recognised Melissa and Penelope. Two vases got flowers before the girls pivoted and dashed for the bathroom. They disappeared from view for a few seconds before Melissa emerged alone, her legs pumping furiously to carry her up the hill. She poured her clamshell of water into her vase, then went back for more.

Penelope ambled into sight, arms outstretched like a zombie. Jason laughed out loud when he recognised the arrangement of shells balanced along her arms. She wasn't just a good cook – she'd served at banquets, too. Steadily, she ascended the hill with her burden, skilfully tipping the contents into her vase. It might not be chess, but strategy seemed to be important in this particular competition. Jason only wished Paige had found a way to include the mud wrestling. After all, she'd incorporated everything else.

Jason grew bored, watching the endless relay of women and water, until one of the girls didn't return to the bottom of the hill. Lorelei waited for the other girls to go down, while she plucked at the hem of her shorts. When she was alone, she crouched between the cameraman and the vases, hiding two of them from sight. The lens panned to follow the rest of the girls labouring up the hill, but a triumphant shout brought Lorelei into focus, holding a filled vase above her head.

Penelope's shells dropped to the sand as she lowered her arms, before charging right for Lorelei. Screeching something unintelligible, Penelope punched Lorelei in the face and they both went down, the vase emptying over them both.

Jason got his mud wrestling as the two girls rolled around in the damp sand, screeching and slapping and pulling each other's hair.

A scream from out of the field of view made the cameraman jump, the footage jerking up with him, before he zoomed in on Melissa. She mumbled something about a bee before the video ended abruptly.

Paige pounded her fist into the table. "Damn it! There's nothing!"

"I don't know," Jason drawled, grinning. "That was a pretty solid jab from Penelope. I wouldn't have pegged her as a fighter, but it looks like she's had some practice. And you said mud wrestling wasn't a good idea."

"It wasn't," she replied through gritted teeth. "Because of those two, we don't have anything from before the bee sting. Not even the bloody bee. The other camera got plenty of footage on the first aid and stuff, but not the initial injury. I interviewed the girls afterwards, but none of them saw it, either. They kept saying how shocked and upset they were at Melissa getting hurt. Well, except for Penelope. She blamed the whole thing on the other girl. Lorelei. The one who won."

"The one who cheated, you mean," Jason said.

"That's what Penelope said, but Lorelei denies it. She said she thought the vase was hers and while she might have mixed them up at first, she's adamant that she didn't that time."

"And which one would you believe?" Jason asked.

He knew his answer. Lorelei had already lied on tape about having sex with him. At least, he was pretty sure it was a lie. Surely he'd recognise her if he'd had her before. He might not remember every girl's name, but he remembered faces. And voices. But he didn't know hers.

Penelope, now that was different. He knew he'd seen her before. Fairly certain he'd slept with her before. She was the only one who hadn't looked surprised when Paige had introduced him as their rock star bachelor. But the way her body reacted when he touched her…no, she wasn't hiding secrets like Lorelei was.

Paige shrugged. "Does it really matter? You're going to go on dates with the girls anyway, and we don't have time to film it all again. Lorelei's the winner, and if we cut that fight scene, her triumph will flow nicely into your date with her in two days' time. You two will take a helicopter to Woody Creek Pearl Farm, cruise the creek and the farm until sunset, maybe spot the local crocodile, Nigel, then have a seafood banquet specially prepared for you by the chef at their restaurant. They promised you'd get to open some of their pearl oysters and keep anything you find inside, too, so I'm not surprised she picked that one. She could be wearing a million dollar pearl to your wedding, if you're lucky."

Jason doubted it. He'd spent enough time talking to the pearl farmers. They wouldn't open the top grade oysters for tourists. They'd be lucky to get jewellery quality pearls at all. But let the girl believe what she liked. Not like she was particularly truthful in what she told everyone else.

That nagging doubt wouldn't leave him alone. Time. He needed more time to get to know her, to get to know all of them better.

"What's on for tomorrow, then?" he asked.

"I have paperwork to fill out for the studio," Paige said sourly. "So we don't get sued for negligence. As if we could keep bees out of an outdoor bush site. But the corporate types in Sydney don't see it that way."

"You have fun with your paperwork, then. I think I'll charter a plane and head inland." Jason felt a grin lifting his lips. He had the perfect spot in mind.

"What? Where? Who with?" Paige demanded.

"Dunno. I figure I'll make it a surprise tomorrow when I tell the girls." He strode out, his mind whirling with ideas.

"Make sure you take one of my cameramen with you! You can't have them all, you know! You have to pick one. Not even you get to have a harem!" Paige called after him. "And don't forget your date with Calais this afternoon!"

Jason's grin widened. He never forgot a date.

FORTY-FIVE

Since Calais got back to camp after her date with Jay, she hadn't stopped smiling. It was getting on Penny's nerves.

To make matters worse, Lorelei strutted around the place like someone had crowned her queen. Penny's punch hadn't broken her nose, though it had split open Penny's knuckles, so Penny had come out of the fight with more injuries than the bitch who started it.

It figured. The universe didn't like her much.

So when a jet boat roared into the cove, and Penny heard Jay shout a cheery good morning, she didn't rise from her seat by the darkened fire pit.

"Perfect day for a trip up north. You want to come with me?"

Penny lifted her eyes to Jay's face. Yes, he was talking to her. Her heart swelled. Maybe something could go right today. "I'd love to," she breathed.

"Where are the others?" Jay asked.

Penny shrugged. "After breakfast, Lorelei went to put her makeup on. That usually takes half the morning. And Calais…I think she went for a walk up to the old pearling camp."

"I'm back! I'm here!" Calais came barrelling down the track, breathless and grinning. "I saw the boat arrive. Is your business at the resort finished for a while? Are you staying with us in the camp again?" So much for the shy girl she'd been. Had Jay popped her cherry last night?

Jay winked. "Maybe. But right now, I have a helicopter waiting on the landing pad at the pearl farm, packed with a picnic lunch, ready for adventure. Are you up for it?"

"Absolutely!" Calais beamed.

"Where's the other girl?" Jay asked.

Calais' face fell. "Lorelei? She's in the bathroom. I'll go get her, if you want."

"Tell her she has five minutes to get in the boat with Baz and the rest of us, or we'll leave her behind," Jay advised.

Calais nodded and trudged to the bathroom.

A cameraman stuck his head out of the crew cabin. "Paige will kill me if I don't come along. All dates have to be recorded." He grabbed his gear and lugged it to the fire pit, where he stood beside Penny, expectantly.

So not just a private adventure for two. All four of them, complete with the fucking photographer.

The universe could go fuck itself. Up the arse with a cactus.

FORTY-SIX

Crammed into a tiny cabin, being heartily sick into a bag whenever the pilot felt the need to fly them through another tight turn, Penny wished she'd stayed back in camp. She hated flying and helicopters were the worst.

Still, she had to admit, the view wasn't too bad out the front window. A multi-layered waterfall trickled from the river at the top of the cliff, through a bunch of tiered lakes to where the river twisted away, far below. If only the river didn't resemble pea soup. Penny's stomach rebelled at the thought of food, so she hunched over a fresh bag.

Good thing, too, as the helicopter spiralled down to land.

Penny was the first out of the helicopter, not stopping until she was more than a dozen metres from those deadly rotors. She wondered if there was any other way to get home. She'd gladly sit here and wait for it. Anything not to have to get back into that helicopter again.

"Can we swim here?" Calais asked eagerly, looking from Jay to the pilot.

Jay nodded. "Sure. There are crocodiles in the river at the bottom, but until they work out how to fly or swim up a cliff, it's safe above the last set of falls."

"Come on." Calais waved to Penny. "Come peek over the lip of the falls with me."

Helicopters and now heights? Penny had had her fill of frightening things. She shook her head.

Calais lowered her voice. "You got some sick on you in the helicopter. At least come to the river to wash it off."

Penny examined her shirt, then eyed the river. "It's green."

"So are you. Come on, it'll help. I promise. You'll feel much better if you just wash your face. You don't have to drink it."

Sighing, Penny followed Calais to the river, where she made a show of splashing plenty of water on her face, neck and her manky shirt. She was surprised to find it did make her feel better. Refreshed, even.

Calais laughed. "See? I told you. Now come check out the view."

"Shouldn't we keep close to the helicopter, so we don't get lost?" Penny suggested, edging away from the cliff even as Calais splashed toward it.

"Wait until Lorelei's discovered we're too far from civilisation for her heels to be any use," Calais said. "And Jay and the pilot have unpacked our picnic. Don't forget that."

Penny would happily have forgotten. She wouldn't be

hungry until the helicopter had flown her home. But she'd spent enough time catering for this lot, with little thanks for her labours. Except from Jay, of course. Let someone else do the work for once.

So she stayed by the river, watching Calais admiring the view, until she heard Jay calling their names.

Lorelei was perched on a picnic blanket, frothing champagne glass in hand. She shot a sour glance at the returned explorers. She'd evidently wanted Jay to herself.

Well, tough titties, bitch, Penny thought. She wouldn't let Lorelei get her claws into Jay.

The others had lunch while Penny looked on, sipping a drink in the shade, as far from the food as possible.

When Jay insisted he was going for a swim, Lorelei leaped to her feet, clapping her hands. Penny and Calais exchanged glances and moved to join them. Instead of leading the way to the river, though, Jay chose a track at the other end of the clearing. One which led steeply downhill.

With a, "Ladies first," Jay let Lorelei lead the way down, assuring them they couldn't get lost because the track didn't branch off until the bottom, which was the river, anyway. Calais, then Penny followed, with Jay bringing up the rear.

Lorelei might not be wearing heels, but her rhinestone-encrusted thongs weren't the most practical shoes for hiking. They slowed her down considerably as she slipped, slid and squawked all the way down the track. Penny would have given her a push so she'd break her silly neck at any one of a dozen points, but Calais was more patient. Or maybe she didn't think she was strong enough to push Lorelei over.

Lorelei's thongs slapped down on wet rock. "It's the

bottom of the waterfall!" she exclaimed, loud enough for them all to hear.

When they all stood at the bottom together, Jay strode past them toward the sheer cliff. "The best swimming hole's up here." He began to climb.

Penny couldn't help but stare. Sure, she knew Jay had a sexy body, but the way he worked those muscles, hauling himself from handhold to handhold, using just his bulging biceps. Or whatever those arm muscles were called.

"Watch out below!" Jay dropped his sneakers, socks and shirt over the cliff, and Calais rushed to save them before they ended up in the river. Next, he whipped off his shorts and they fluttered down, too. "It's just us here, and the water's warm. Come up for a skinnydip. First one to reach my pool can have me." He disappeared from view.

Calais settled on the rock beside Jay's things. "I'm fine here, thanks."

"More fool you, then!" Lorelei cried, clawing her way up to a ledge a third of the way up the cliff.

Swimming naked in a slimy, green river with who knew what in it? Not to mention the cameraman still at the top of the falls, where he could be watching and recording everything. Penny wanted Jay, but not like that. However, if Lorelei wanted to fall and break her neck, all by herself, Penny wanted a front row seat. Decision made, Penny took a seat beside Calais.

"Anyone coming, or am I swimming up here by myself again?" Jay called. He stood on the ledge, proud and jutting and just as big as Penny remembered.

"Oh God!" Calais squeezed her eyes shut.

Lorelei squealed in delight. "Holy shit, it's huge, Jay. I'm coming!" She scrabbled at the edge and rolled her body over the top. With a cry of triumph, she peeled off her clothes and piled them on the cliff edge, setting her candy-pink g-string in pride of place on top. She disappeared from sight, but unfortunately, they could still hear her, loud and clear.

"Will it fit?" Lorelei cried.

Penny wanted to vomit again.

"For someone who's supposedly had so much sex with Jay, she sounded really surprised to see all of him," Calais remarked.

Penny paused. "You mean, you think she was lying about all the things she'd done with him?" It figured. Lying, cheating bitch.

"Oh yes. I find it hard to believe a word she says sometimes I mean, her career as an international model? I never heard of her. And all the famous people she said she knows? Jay doesn't know her, either. I asked. He said he'd never met her before the speed dating session at the resort."

Penny snorted. "So that's what you two were doing last night? You spent your whole date with Jay discussing her?" She couldn't bring herself to name the bitch.

Calais blushed. "No, though we did spend a lot of it talking. He's so nice, and so easy to talk to. I never intended to tell him half of what I did, but it just sort of came out. About life on my family's farm, and my sister..." She laughed shakily. "I never talk about her. Not to anyone. It still hurts too much. But with Jay, it was so easy. And he understood, like he knew what it was like to lose someone so close to you. The worry when you don't hear from them, the slow decline until...they're gone."

"Cancer?" Penny asked.

Calais shook her head. "She was in an abusive relationship, and she died. Suicide, they told me, but from what I saw of the boyfriend, I'm not sure. Either he drove her to it or he did it. I remember when they met. She adored him. Wouldn't hear a word said wrong about him. And now I'll never know what she thought of him at the end. She didn't even leave a note. Not for me, not for anyone."

"That…must be hard," Penny managed to say. What did you say to someone who'd lost someone to suicide, or maybe murder? Everything she thought of sounded so trite.

"It was. It still is. Especially wishing there was something I could have done to save her. But she wouldn't let me. She loved him too much, and it killed her." Calais' laughter turned bitter. "They say love hurts, but not that it kills. When people talk about how powerful it is, they don't say how it can destroy. Like a force of nature. Like this river must be when it floods in the wet season."

Penny didn't want to imagine the river in the wet season. Swirling floodwaters, swollen with cyclonic rains, that would sweep them away like leaves on the wind.

"But love's a good thing," Penny argued, thinking of the thrill she got when Jay touched her. That she wanted more of. That the fucking bitch up there shouldn't be getting.

"Not always."

"So you're not here for love?" Penny challenged. Calais had to be lying.

Calais sighed. "No, I'm not. Look, don't get me wrong. Jay's awesome. It was worth it just to meet him. He's like the perfect big brother you always wished you had. Not that

I don't love my brother – I do. And he's awesome, too. But Jay…he's like having a superhero for a brother. He's not the sort of guy either of us is likely to meet normally. But somehow we did and he's just…perfect. Don't you think?"

Moaning and squealing sounded from above.

"Sounds like your Mr Perfect is having sex with Lorelei. That knocks his halo right off, in my book," Penny remarked.

"Only if I wanted him for myself. He's only doing it to be nice, you know. He said he's too soft-hearted to turn a girl down. Doesn't want her to feel bad about herself, so if he can, he does. He's gone to so much trouble to make this trip memorable for us." Calais waved at the falls. "I mean, just look at this place!" She froze, staring at the crocodile warning sign. "Are there really crocodiles here, or was he joking about that?"

Penny pointed across the river, where two metre-long beasts were sunning themselves on a rock. "You could ask Penny Croc and Calais Croc over there."

Calais squinted at the crocodiles. "They don't look very big. If those are the babies, where's their mum?"

"Nah, those are freshwater ones. They won't hurt you. I don't think they get much bigger than that. It's the salties that eat people. Those are what you have to watch out for."

Calais stared at her. "Did you used to live up here? You know so much about them."

Penny nodded. "Hedland, then here. Or Broome, at least. Before I joined a cruise ship to cook my way around the world. At first, I laughed about crocodiles being an important part of the safety briefing, but that was before I saw one of the big ones. They're fast and deadly. If they get their teeth into you, you're a goner."

They sat there in silence for a few minutes, before Calais said softly, "We can't let Lorelei get her teeth into Jay. He doesn't deserve someone like her. I don't know who he'll send home next. If it's me, can you promise me something? If it comes down to just you and her, don't let him choose her."

"I swear," Penny said instantly. "Same, though. If he sends me home and it's just you and her, don't let the bitch have him."

"Deal," Calais said.

They both watched as a bright green bottom appeared over the edge, bisected by a pink g-string. Penny and Calais fought not to laugh as Lorelei, her back covered in slime from crown to knees, climbed down the cliff. When she reached the bottom she turned to face the other two girls, fanning her flushed face. "Oh my God, that was incredible," she said. "Like having a jackhammer inside me. You can't imagine what it feels like." She smirked. "We're going to have one incredible wedding night. You'll have to watch it on TV, seeing as you won't be invited." It took her a moment to realise what she'd said. "To the wedding. You won't be invited to the wedding. And there won't be cameras on the wedding night. I'd never sink so low as to need to do porn films!"

Calais managed not to laugh, but Penny wasn't that polite. "Yeah, good luck with that," Penny said. The only way Lorelei would be Jay's bride was over her dead body. And now, Calais', too. The bitch didn't stand a chance.

FORTY-SEVEN

For the next few days following the trip to the falls, Penny and Calais avoided Lorelei as much as possible, leaving her at the camp with Bec and Luke while they hiked up to the bluff and watched for whales. Calais had spotted a couple before Penny saw a single one, but more and more were swimming past, heading for the other side of the archipelago, to their breeding grounds.

Jay remained at the resort, not staying at the camp at all, to Penny's dismay. That meant he wasn't with Lorelei, though, which was a good thing. He'd collected her for their date and returned her right after, with a casual wave to the other girls before he headed back to the resort by boat.

But when Paige arrived, with two new cameramen in tow, Penny paid attention. She and Calais spotted the boat in the distance, so they had time to make their way to the beach in time to meet the boat. "Time for the family dinner," Paige said, trudging up the beach. "Are you feeling nervous yet?"

Calais' jaw dropped. "We get to meet Jay's family?"

Paige shrugged. "Standard part of the show. The bachelors get to show the girls off and get outside opinions from the people they know and trust. More work for me, because I have to interview anyone who's willing to offer an opinion, but this is where things get mixed up a bit, because they usually see things Jay won't, because they're not in looooove."

Penny couldn't help but smile. No member of Jay's family would want him anywhere near Lorelei. She and Calais had a chance, though, if they played their cards right. Mums and grandmas always loved a girl who could cook, something Penny had in the bag. Calais would probably just clam up, which suited Penny fine.

"Traditionally, this is where you girls get to cook for them all, too, but because dinner's at the resort, I'm not sure. Jay will let us know when we arrive." She clapped her hands. "Chop chop! Get your things, girls. You're moving back to the resort for the night. We'll be back at camp tomorrow, though. Can't have you getting too cosy."

FORTY-EIGHT

Penny almost moaned at the sheer pleasure of having a hot shower again. It had been weeks. Not that the camp showers had been cold, but…it just wasn't the same. So she missed civilisation. She was a city girl – she was supposed to. For the first time, she looked forward to the end of filming, just so she could have all the everyday comforts she missed. Like hot water, a fridge, an oven, electric lights, not having to restrain herself from killing Lorelei in her sleep…

Reluctantly, she turned off the taps and stepped out of the shower, wondering what to wear. She'd brought two dresses for the trip – both more suitable for dates than family dinners. One of them would have to do, though, seeing as there wasn't a clothing shop on the island and the souvenir shop only sold swimsuits, board shorts and t-shirts.

The black or the blue? That decision was easy – the

blue, of course. Her little black dress was definitely for dates, and she had one with Jay this week. The blue would have to do.

Hoping she still remembered how to do it, she curled her hair into a twist on the back of her head and secured it with a silver clip that she knew stood out against her dark hair, though she couldn't see it herself. She dug out her makeup and set to work. Not too much – she didn't want his family to think she shovelled it on the way Lorelei did – but just enough to show, so they could see that she'd made an effort to look good. She didn't have much jewellery, so she didn't bother wearing any.

She dug out her heels, which had languished in the bottom of her bag since they'd boarded the boat for Camp Romance, and slipped them onto her feet. It felt strange after so long in flat shoes, so she practised striding across the room in them, until she felt like she wasn't going to trip on every other step. It's not like they were six inches high. They were a fairly modest three, she thought, peering down.

A knock sounded at the door. Was it time already?

"Who is it?" Penny quavered.

"I'm Adam, the hotel porter, ma'am. Reception sent me with a delivery for you."

A porter she didn't know. Penny waved the door open.

He held out a small bag, about the size of his hand. By his side, he held two more.

"Who's it from?" she asked, taking the bag and peering inside.

"Reception, ma'am," he repeated tersely.

Reception. Right. She thanked him and retreated into her room, letting the door hiss closed behind her. Puzzled, she tipped the bag out on the bed. All it contained was a black box, tied shut with a coal-coloured bow. She untied it and tugged off the lid. And gasped.

Inside was a pearl necklace with matching earrings. The pearls were an unusual silvery blue that she'd never seen before, set in brushed silver. Penny held the box up beside her face, staring intently at her reflection in the mirror. They were a perfect match for both her and the dress. Who had sent them? And how had they known?

Deciding that she would wear jewellery after all, she donned the timely gift, tucked a stray wisp of hair behind her ear, and ventured to the Dampier Room for dinner.

FORTY-NINE

Penny smoothed her skirt before walking into the Dampier Room, aware of the cameras recording everything. She breathed a sigh of relief when she saw she wasn't the last to arrive. Aside from the camera crew, there were only three other people present at the table set for eight: Jay, Calais and a woman who looked around Penny's age sat beside Calais. Jay's sister, perhaps?

"Penelope, this is my hotel manager, Xan Lane," Jay said, banishing that idea. "She takes care of the resort while I'm off enjoying myself with you ladies."

Xan rolled her eyes. "I take care of the resort, regardless. I have yet to see you do a day's work since you arrived." She had an English accent, a strong contrast to her tanned, athletic appearance. Penny would have pegged her as Aussie to the core.

Jay grinned. "One of the perks of being the boss."

So Meier had left, to be replaced by…her. Penny shook hands with the woman, wondering how someone so young could get a job managing a place like Romance Island Resort. Not through sleeping with Jay, by the sound of things.

Calais didn't scrub up too badly, Penny decided, eyeing the girl beside Xan. She'd let her hair down and looked like she'd taken advantage of being in civilisation to wash and style it properly, so it fell in soft curls around her face. She smiled at Penny, nervously tucking a curl behind her ear, and Penny saw that she wasn't the only one who'd received pearls. Calais' were a different colour, though – not blue but a pale gold, set in gold instead of silver. She had a matching pendant around her neck, too, that gave her dark, wine-coloured dress a startling splash of brightness.

If Calais got to sit beside Jay, Penny would do the same, she decided, sinking onto the empty chair on Jay's right.

Her bottom had barely touched the cushion before Jay leaned over and whispered, "I take it you liked my gift?"

Penny glanced at her necklace. Not from Reception. From Jay, of course.

"Absolutely. Thank you," she replied.

Jay grinned. "I was bored at the pearl showroom the other night with Lorelei, and I didn't know pearls came in so many colours, instead of just white, so I thought you ladies might like something, too." He looked uncertain. "Are they okay? I don't usually do jewellery, because I don't know what to buy. The girl at the counter picked these out for me when I described you."

How precisely had he described her for a girl she'd never met to pick something so perfect? Oh God, how much had it cost? Penny squirmed in her seat. "It's lovely. Really."

"Good." Jay sighed, glancing around. "Is it just the four of us for dinner? Where's everyone else?"

The seats across the table didn't remain unoccupied for long. The two IT guys crept in to take the seats across from Calais and Xan, followed by Jackie, one of the senior maids Penny remembered from when she worked here. Penny received a nod of recognition from the woman and wanted to sink under the table, but she was forced to smile as Jay made introductions. Just as long as Jackie didn't mention Penny's previous work experience, it would be okay, Penny promised herself.

"Oh, are you here already?" Lorelei sang out, prancing into the room. She wore an over-the-top evening gown that was slit to the waist, showing off her surgically enhanced boobs. Strategically placed clusters of rhinestones held the dress together at shoulder, hip and navel, and Lorelei wore earrings to match, with not a single pearl in sight.

Hadn't Jay bought her jewellery? He'd hated his date that much, that he'd decided to buy gifts for the other girls instead? Penny stifled a grin.

Lorelei's hair looked like a mop that had gotten tangled in the mangroves after a cyclone: half up, half down, with tendrils sticking out like they'd been windblown that way. Penny guessed it must be something fresh out of the latest fashion magazine, because Lorelei didn't look the least bit flustered when everyone stared. "You must be Jay's mother, brothers and sister! I'm delighted to meet you!" Lorelei swanned around the table, shaking hands with Jay's family of staff, oblivious to the coughing fit Jackie faked to cover her laughter.

Jay waited until Lorelei was seated across from him to correct her.

"Oh!" In one syllable and its accompanying sneer, Lorelei managed to convey her complete disgust for anyone who worked in a hotel. Penny wanted to kick her under the table. A normal person would have at least had the grace to look embarrassed at such a stupid mistake, but not Lorelei.

A waiter wandered in with a bottle of champagne and proceeded to fill everyone's glasses. Well, with no vehicles on the island, no one had to be the designated driver tonight, Penny thought, taking a big gulp of her wine. She felt Jackie's eyes on her, so she took another defiant gulp before setting the glass down.

"So what have you been doing with yourself after you left here?" Jackie asked.

Penny opened her mouth to answer.

Lorelei tittered. "Did you used to work here, Penelope?"

"We were both maids together in the Housekeeping department for a season, until Penny left," Jackie said, lifting her wineglass.

"A maid? Now I know where you learned to fight. You must have had to fight off some of the determined male guests, I'm sure. After all, in a place like this, they'd expect full service maids, right?" Lorelei laughed.

Penny wanted to punch her again, but knew she couldn't with the cameras watching.

"Some of the guests have more hormones than sense," Jackie agreed. "But the resort has always had a firm policy on not letting the staff fraternise with guests. Tonight's an exception, of course, because Mr Felix likes to blur the lines. We're all family here, he says."

"Family?" Jay repeated. "Yes, we are. Jackie's my housekeeper, on top of her normal job, so she makes sure I don't burn the place down. Cam and Seb over there make sure we have communications and enough TV channels, so we don't get bored and cause too much trouble, while Xan keeps everyone in line. Even me."

"Bullshit," Xan replied. "No one's managed to keep Jay in line yet. Isn't that why he wants one of you ladies? Making him behave sounds like a wifely duty, for sure."

Calais giggled, but was drowned out by Lorelei's loud laughter.

"I'd be willing to give it a go!" Lorelei exclaimed.

Over my dead body, thought Penny, but she forced a smile for the camera.

"Look, here comes the first course," Xan said. "You should have seen the chefs when I told them you said you wanted a banquet for eight. We had to add a few courses to make sure each of them got to design their own course. Apparently everyone wants to be a celebrity chef and all it takes is one reality TV show to make you famous, or so I hear."

Penny fervently hoped so. The way things were going tonight, with Jay ignoring her to talk to Calais or his staff most of the time, she knew she wouldn't be winning a rock star out of the show. But her own cooking show would be a cool consolation prize…

A resounding clang gonged through the room, drawing everyone's eye to the door. The orange-splattered chef didn't seem to care that he'd dropped his platter, which two waiters scrambled to clean up. No, Patel's eyes were transfixed on Penny.

Lorelei giggled. "He sure looks shocked to see you, Penelope. Do you know the chef, too?"

Feeling everyone's eyes on her, especially Jay's, Penny swallowed. She had to keep cool. "Oh, he's just my ex," she said with what she hoped sounded like nonchalance. "We broke up a year ago. I didn't know he still worked here." A lie, but a necessary one. He hadn't spoken to her since she'd stopped working at the resort, so she'd assumed that meant they were over. But the way he stared at her now, his eyes full of hurt, made her wonder…and Jay had noticed, too.

Fuck. Fuck fuck fuckity fuck.

She spent the next fifteen minutes studiously ignoring Patel, until he left the room and a different chef brought the next course in.

Go fuck yourself, universe, Penny thought, hoping the dinner would be done soon. Oh, and universe? Use two cactuses this time.

FIFTY

Thanking the whole sky full of lucky stars that THAT ordeal was finally over, Penny settled at a pub table to sip her beer, wishing she could have a cigarette. The night was officially a disaster, so she may as well drink herself into oblivion until she could sink into a soft hotel bed.

"Right, how about some fun?" Paige gushed.

Penny swore under her breath. Nothing that woman thought up was her idea of fun. More likely, she'd thought up some fresh torture to put them through. Spin the bottle, a wet t-shirt contest to rival the one at the Roebuck Bay Hotel, a game of bingo...

"Karaoke!" Paige squealed, yanking away a makeshift curtain from the wall, revealing a TV screen.

Great. At least with the wet t-shirt contest, she'd have had an excuse to pour her drink over Lorelei's perfect head. Now, all she could do was hope no one asked her to sing, because she had no musical talent at all.

"Who's first?" Paige scanned the group. Penny deliberately didn't make eye contact. "Aww, c'mon. It'll be fun!"

"I never turn down a chance to sing," Jay said, rising. "Someone pick me a song."

Paige giggled. "Actually, I already programmed a few in, to get the party started." She aimed a remote control at the screen, holding out the microphone for Jay in her other hand. "Something easy to start with."

Jay snorted as the song title came on the screen. Chaya's *Necessary Evil*, their first big hit. He didn't need the words for this one, belting out the words with what Penny thought looked like bitterness. Didn't he like the song? It was one of his, after all.

As the last words died away, Paige shouted, "The next one's a duet. Who's going to sing with our rock star?"

Penny shook her head, tightening her grip on her pint. Calais refused, too. Lorelei was nowhere to be seen — probably repainting her face in the toilets, Penny decided. She wondered what would happen when the girl ran out of makeup at the beach camp. Or maybe her suitcase was full of the stuff, so she'd be able to hide behind her mask for months, if need be.

The magic carpet song from *Aladdin* came on, and Penny fought not to laugh. A Disney duet? Hardly suitable for a rock star. Not even Jay would be able to pull off a proper performance, if he didn't know the words.

Yet he did, his voice soaring through the male part as effortlessly as if the part had been written for him. When the female part appeared on the screen, he offered the microphone to Calais, then Penny, but both refused, again. He shrugged, grinned, and launched into the funniest falsetto Penny had ever heard.

"Princess Jay-smine!" Paige hooted, clapping.

Penny found herself sniggering, then outright laughing, as Jay fluttered his eyelashes like an experienced drag queen. Wait, was he?

No, he couldn't be. He'd risen to fame when he was only eighteen or nineteen – barely legal age to go into any of the clubs in Kings Cross, let alone become a seasoned performer in one. And everyone knew how much he loved women.

Someone slammed a glass on the table behind Penny, dragging her attention from Jay.

"I knew I'd seen you before!" Cam exclaimed. "You're the accounts girl from Hookers Real Estate!"

Lorelei turned white. "Nah, that's not me," she said, her eyes darting every which way like the lying bitch she was.

"Yeah. I'd know that butterfly anywhere." Cam pointed at the tattoo spread across Lorelei's clearly visible cleavage. "Even if those are bigger than I remember. Did you get a boob job? They look awesome." He stared avidly at Lorelei's breasts.

"No, you must have mixed me up with someone else. I – "

Cam grabbed Seb's arm. "Hey, mate. Doesn't she look like the girl from Hookers?"

Seb turned and squinted at Lorelei. "Nah, the girl from Hookers disappeared, remember? I had to hack her accounts for the police, when they were trying to find her. The investigation ended when they found out she'd left the country."

Cam grinned. "Yeah, to get a boob job, looks like. Don't you think she has incredible tits now?"

Seb seemed less enthusiastic about them. "Very nice." He turned his attention back to Jay's performance.

"So is that why you got the implants? For the show?" Cam asked eagerly.

Lorelei squirmed in her seat, to Penny's delight. Her discomfort only lasted a moment before she jumped up and exclaimed, "Oh, that's my song!' She trotted up to take the microphone from Jay.

Penny ignored Lorelei's simpering rendition of some mass-produced pop song to focus on the IT guys' discussion behind her.

"You shouldn't have scared her off like that. I was this close, man!" Cam held his fingers millimetres apart.

Seb glanced around, as if making sure they weren't overheard. "The accounts girl from Hookers ripped them off for a fortune. She was stealing from all the client accounts, transferring the money into an offshore account. It wasn't until she left that someone noticed, and they needed me to unlock her profile. If she isn't the same girl, you're the one who scared her off, and if she is…she wouldn't want us knowing, would she?"

Cam looked stricken. "But if she is…you think she's after Mr Felix's money? Shouldn't we tell him?"

"Tell me what, guys?" Jay asked easily, flopping into the chair beside Penny without spilling a drop of his beer. "I should sing for Disney? 'Cause I'm not taking her as a backup singer." He jerked his head at Lorelei, who was now bumping and grinding to a song from *The Little Mermaid.*

Ugh.

"No, you shouldn't. We think…we think she did the same thing as Meier. Ripped off her employer and disappeared. Or she looks like a chick who did." Seb gave a tight smile. "What should we do?"

Jay shrugged. "Mention it to Xan. She's friends with one of the police constables in town. They don't like me much. She'll sort it and see if Lorelei is a criminal or just looks a lot like one." He drank deeply, then slammed his half-empty glass on the table. "Right. This song's mine, and you're doing it with me." He grabbed Penny's hand and hauled her up to the front.

She protested, but she was too shocked at what she'd heard to put much energy into resisting. Lorelei, wanted by the law? Oh, this was too good. To be rid of her biggest adversary by getting the bitch arrested…tonight was looking up.

"Summer loving!" Jay shouted as he handed Penny a microphone.

What? The music started, and Penny recognised the *Grease* medley. At least it was something she vaguely knew. Jay's arm slid around her waist. "The words are on the screen if you forget them, and there aren't any cameras tonight. Copyright of the songs or whatever. Even if they did film this, they couldn't show it on TV. Just relax and have fun." He winked and launched into the song like he'd sung it a hundred times before.

He even had the John Travolta dance moves. Penny stood there, mesmerised, until he pointed at the screen. Her turn to sing. Oh, right.

Penny managed to mangle her lines before the medley

mercifully moved on to *Greased Lightning*. Good thing it was completely Jay's part for a bit, because that hip thrust, arse wiggle combo he had going on meant she wasn't staring at any boring screen.

Wait…what? Oh, her turn to sing again. That *Summer Nights* duet thing. Flustered, she fixed her gaze on the screen and tried to remember how the song went. Jay's arm around her didn't make it any easier, but he didn't move away, so she figured she must have done okay.

At the end, he let go of her to applaud her performance, and Penny clumsily clapped right back. God, she'd be dreaming of him tonight. What would it feel like if he did that hip thrust on top of her…or behind her…or…anywhere, anytime.

She sank into a seat before her weak knees gave out.

What felt like only a few minutes later, Paige announced the evening's entertainment was over, and Penny rose. Calais was already on her feet, smothering a yawn. Lorelei was nowhere in sight. Maybe she'd done a runner, Penny gloated. If she hadn't, someone had to tell the police about her.

FIFTY-ONE

When the sun rose, Penny had already made her decision. She wouldn't call the police, because that's not how things were done at Romance Island Resort, something that had been drummed into her long ago when she'd worked here as a lowly maid. No, she'd dump this mess in the lap of that new manager and let her handle it. That way, Penny wouldn't be implicated if Lorelei got arrested, so Penny wouldn't look bad in front of all the viewers when the show went to air. She wasn't a tattle-tale like that righteous bitch Audra.

Her thongs slapped against the soles of her feet as she marched across the foyer to the manager's office. Mr Meier had always kept the door closed, forcing you to knock and wait for permission to enter. This new manager kept the door wide open, so Penny didn't need to knock to get the woman's attention. Her eyes were already firmly fixed on her visitor.

"Yes?" the manager asked.

"I'm…Penelope. One of the girls here for…the show," Penny began. "Look, I couldn't help overhearing last night, but two of the staff here were talking about one of the other girls on the show. They said she looked like – "

"A criminal?" the manager interrupted. "You're the fourth person this morning to tell me. Turns out Lorelei is none other than Brooke Barnett, wanted for stealing as a servant, taking thousands of dollars from the company she worked for. What made her think she could hide on a reality TV show is beyond me, but some people are just plain stupid, I guess. And you might want to pack your things, just in case the show gets cancelled over this. Jay just left to find the production manager, to give her a piece of his mind."

No. They couldn't cancel the show. This was her only chance to get her reputation back.

"Where is she?" Penny asked.

The manager shrugged. "She set up shop in one of the conference rooms. The Sunset Room, I think."

Penny nodded her thanks and hurried out. She had to distract Jay – stop him before he could ruin this for her.

FIFTY-TWO

"Is this one big joke to you?" Jason demanded, striding into the conference room.

Paige jumped, spilling her coffee. She looked tired, Jason was glad to see.

"Laying the drama on thick for the show. Playing me like a fucking idiot. I promised you a finale to remember, but you lied. No criminals. No one wanted by the police. And you tried to set me up with a thief. An unprincipled bitch who steals from the people who trust her." Jason hadn't been this angry since he found out what Gaia had done to Flavia. No, since he'd jumped out of a fucking helicopter. "Answer me, or get the fuck off my island. The deal is over. You can stick your show up your boss's arse."

Paige mumbled something unintelligible.

Through clenched teeth, Jason insisted she repeat it. Louder.

"I didn't know," she whispered.

"Bullshit."

"I didn't!" Paige protested. "Someone in the studio handles background checks for guests on the show. I don't know how they missed this. Maybe they didn't have time to check, or maybe she gave a fake name, or..."

"Yeah, she gave a fake name, all right. Lorelei, instead of bloody Brooke. An accounts payable clerk, not a model, like she said she was. What other bullshit have you tried to sell me that I don't know about yet?"

The panic in Paige's eyes confirmed Jason's suspicions. She hadn't known about Lorelei/Brooke/bitch-who-was-leaving-his-island-right-now, but she was hiding something. "The...the ring," she squeaked.

"What ring?"

"I mentioned to the jewellers in town that it might be good advertising for them if one of their pieces was used in the show's finale, if there was a proposal. One of them came through. The hotel manager has it in her safe – I didn't trust the room safes for something that expensive. It's more than I earn in a year." Paige swallowed. "That's the only thing I haven't told you. I've been straight with you from the beginning, I swear. You've had access to all the show footage, just like I promised. We have to finish the show." Now she looked terrified.

Jason's anger ebbed. Sure, he was pissed off, but he hadn't meant to scare her. What did she think he'd do, hit her? Not fucking likely. "You want to line up those three girls tonight so I can send one home? I don't think so. I don't want that girl on my island for another minute. Get rid of her. Take her to the police lockup where scum like her belongs."

"But…you have to be there. To look shocked at —"

Jason shook his head. "You don't want me swearing on your show, and I have nothing to say to the girl. Get rid of her, and maybe I'll still agree to do the final proposal, like we discussed. Maybe."

Were those tears in Paige's eyes? Jason softened a little more.

"But our date! What about our date?" a new voice cried.

Penelope stumbled into the room, wild-eyed. "I'm still supposed to have a date with you. I want to make a meal for you in front of the film crew."

Great. Now Jason had two crying women. "All right, one date. That's all."

"And the finale. When you choose the girl you like best," Paige piped up hopefully.

"Yeah, whatever," Jason grumbled, throwing his hands into the air. "Just get rid of her." He stalked out.

FIFTY-THREE

Penny stared at Paige, before the production manager held out a box of tissues. They both said nothing while they wiped their tears away and blew their noses, but the tension in the room hadn't left with Jay. If anything, it had intensified.

"What's going to happen with the show?" Penny ventured.

Paige took a deep breath, summoning back some of the hardness she normally exhibited. "The show must go on. You heard him. You two have a date, and then he'll…make his choice." A crafty smile appeared on Paige's lips. "He won't do what he's supposed to, and send her away like a normal elimination. The viewers won't understand why, though. We have to handle this right. How much do you know?" Calculating eyes evaluated Penny over Paige's cup of coffee.

"That Lorelei isn't who she says she is, and she's wanted by the police," Penny said slowly, hoping it was the right response.

"Does the other girl – Calais. Does she know?"

Penny shook her head. "I don't think so."

"What would it take for you to forget what you know for a few hours, so you look properly shocked when the police come to arrest her?"

Money. Fame. Jay. "I want you not to make me into the show's bitch when it goes to air," Penny blurted out.

Paige choked out a laugh. "The show's bitch?"

Penny reddened. "Every reality TV show has a bitch. Someone the audience loves to hate. Make it Lorelei, not me. Even if I don't…don't win."

"You don't think he'll pick you, either," Paige said. "What are you in this for, then?"

It was now or never. Penny took a deep breath. "I'm a chef. Or at least, an apprentice one. I want to finish my apprenticeship with one of the best, but they'll never take me on. What I need is an edge. To be famous for my cooking. I want a spot on a cooking show, or one of the contests. Like the one you usually host when you're not matchmaking rock stars." She let out a breath she hadn't even known she'd been holding, but she didn't dare uncross her fingers. She needed all the luck she could get. Paige would never go for it. Penny was asking too much.

Paige regarded Penny, then nodded once. "All right. You and Calais and Lorelei, dress up for today's elimination as if nothing had happened. And no matter what happens once the cameras start rolling, you act like it's a bigger surprise than the rock star you want, the day you first found out his name."

"Deal," Penny said, hoping the woman would keep her word. Her stomach roiled uneasily. After all, in the TV industry, what was her word worth? Either of them could be lying. Maybe even both.

If she was, then Penny had only one way to win in this show. She had to win not just the viewers' hearts, but Jay's as well. Jay would help her fulfil her dream, she was sure of it. Jay had to choose her instead of Calais.

Calais, who'd been her ally against Lorelei since the beginning.

But all was fair in love and war, Penny reasoned. And when it came to Jay's love, it definitely was war. To the death, if need be.

FIFTY-FOUR

Paige lined all three of them up on the lagoon beach, in a secluded spot you didn't see from the path until you were there. That meant you couldn't see anyone creeping up on you, either, Penny knew, but she didn't have anything to hide. It's not like she was making out with anyone on the beach. Not today, anyway.

Lorelei wore a triumphant smile, glancing sideways at Penny as if she knew a particularly juicy secret.

Penny wanted to punch through those perfectly capped teeth, break that surgically shaped nose and kick the bitch in her silicon enhanced boobs. But with the cameras rolling, she couldn't let her face say that. Instead, she kept her head down, intent on smoothing the sand with her toes. She hoped she looked more apprehensive than angry. If Lorelei wasn't going to be arrested today, Penny might have been eliminated by Jay instead.

Now who had a juicy secret? Penny forced herself not to smile, hugging her delicious knowledge to herself.

"Where's Mr Felix?" one of the cameramen asked.

The others shrugged.

"Bloody humid out here. Too hot to wait in the sun for him."

Faintly, Penny heard the whine of a jet boat. The police, she hoped. That meant Lorelei wouldn't have the luxury of a helicopter ride to jail. No, she'd have a rough jetboat ride during which she'd almost definitely get soaked and seasick, before the police drove her down the red, rough-as-hell gravel road back to town. She smiled at her toes, deciding that the chipped polish should be redone tonight to celebrate Lorelei…no, Brooke…getting her just desserts. *Karma's a bitch, baby, and none deserve it more than you,* she thought.

Time stretched interminably, as perspiration trickled between her shoulder blades while she stood in the hot sun, wishing she'd brought a hat or something she could use to fan herself. Would the film crew tell her off for going to stand in the shade?

Penny glanced over and met Paige's hard gaze, firmly fixed on her. No, Paige was watching her every move. No rest for the indebted. Penny sighed. It would be worth it if Paige came through. All she had to do was cook Jay the perfect meal on their date tonight and she'd have everything she could ever want. Him, her reputation back, and happiness.

Maybe she'd even offer Jay a blowjob for dessert. That's how Lorelei had seduced him – with sex. Two could play at that game. Or one, seeing as Brooke's time on the island was ticking away. Victory was Penny's, she knew it. Shy Calais didn't stand a chance.

Steps crunched on the path, and a cameraman backed into view. The hotel manager marched onto the sand next, wearing a particularly grim expression. Behind her strode two equally grim-faced police officers.

Penny's mouth dropped open in genuine shock. The two hulking men weren't locals from the station in town. Last time she was here, the Cape Leveque Road patrol had a woman on it. If she'd ever seen either of these men before, she'd have volunteered to be arrested.

"Brooke Burnett, otherwise known as Lorelei Lovekiss, you're under arrest," one uniformed, muscle-bound hottie said.

Calais gave an audible gasp. "She's what?"

Brooke managed a shaky laugh. "You're joking. You have me mixed up with someone else. I'm not this other girl. Brooke? Whatever her name is. I haven't stolen anything or killed anybody. I've done nothing wrong!" Her voice ended in a hysterical shriek as Hottie Number Two snapped handcuffs on her wrists.

"We can discuss that at the station, miss," he said.

Bracketing her like the world's most drool-worthy bookends, they each took one of Brooke's arms and escorted her back the way they'd arrived.

One cameraman followed them, but the other kept his lens on Penny and Calais.

As soon as they were out of sight, Penny let her breath hiss out. The hard bit was over – she hadn't given the game away to Brooke. Now, she had to play her part until Paige was satisfied.

"Oh my God, was that real?" Penny asked Calais. "Were those real police officers?"

Calais sniffled, wiping away tears. "Yes. Detectives from Perth. The last time I saw that uniform, was when they came to my house to tell us about my sister…"

Her sister had been arrested for something horrible, too? Then Penny remembered: Calais' sister was dead. She wrapped her arms around Calais in what she hoped looked like a sympathetic hug. She tried to keep the triumph off her face, but it was hard. After all, Lorelei was gone.

Calais clung to her for what felt like ages, until the jet boat roared into life and headed off. The cameraman returned, and Paige directed Penny to a spot under a tree, where she was required to babble endlessly about how shocked she was about Lorelei's arrest, her hopes for her relationship with Jay and how she felt terribly betrayed by being so close to a criminal all this time. Penny summoned her best worried look as she said she hoped Jay wouldn't take his favourite's defection too hard. Not that she called Lorelei Jay's favourite. God, no. That was loser talk. And she was no loser. Not this time. No, this time, Penny was going to be the winner who takes all, because, by God, she deserved it this time. Finally, things were going right.

FIFTY-FIVE

It felt surprisingly comfortable to be back at Camp Romance, putting on her lipstick in front of the tiny bathroom mirror. Penny wanted to dance. Finally, she was getting her date with Jay. And not just any date. A romantic dinner, followed by an evening together in a luxury tent. One with electricity and a king-sized bed. If everything went right, that bed would come in very handy for showing Jay just how compatible they were, in every way. Calais couldn't compete with that.

Penny climbed behind the wheel of the old four-wheel-drive, careful to avoid brushing the rust spots, which would show on her dress. She turned the key and instead of rumbling to life, the engine clicked. She wrenched at the key again, but got the same response.

Oh God. What was wrong with the car? She was supposed to meet Jay at the pearl farm. He'd be waiting for her. This couldn't happen now.

"Luke!" she called, hoping the camp manager was around and hadn't gone fishing. "What's wrong with the car?"

"Nothing's wrong with the car," he said, taking a long pull on his beer and settling deeper into his chair on the veranda.

"It won't start! There is something wrong with it," Penny insisted. "I'm supposed to be at the pearl farm in a few minutes, with that car."

It took ten minutes of alternately begging and threatening to get Luke of his lazy arse and into the driver's seat.

He turned the key, coaxing more clicks out of the car, then climbed out again. "Flat battery. It won't start."

Penny's heart sank. "Don't we have spare batteries? I'm sure I saw one in the kitchen. It had one of those portable fridges running off it."

"Nah, don't know what you're talking about," Luke drawled, taking another drink.

Penny's temper rose. "It was full of those beers last time I looked, no food at all. Where is it now?" She scanned the kitchen, but the cooler was gone. "Where is it?" she repeated.

Bec marched up the veranda, drawn to the brewing argument. "Are you looking for Luke's beer fridge? He hooked it up to the car battery this morning, when the others went flat. It'll be in the shade beside one of the front tyres."

"The car battery's flat, too," Penny said.

That got Bec's attention. "What? I'm supposed to head

into town in the morning to get more supplies. You mean we're stuck here?"

"I need to get to the pearl farm today before dark. We better not be stuck here." Penny glared at Luke.

Luke didn't look the slightest bit repentant. "So radio for help, then. Or go for a walk."

"The radio needs batteries, you fool," Bec said through gritted teeth. "And it's miles to the pearl farm. In the dark. With wild bulls in the bush. And snakes."

Luke shrugged. "Not my problem. I have all the beer I need to do me 'til morning."

Bec looked as furious as Penny felt.

"You won't have a job by morning. If I have to walk to the farm, I'll call the office and tell them what you did. That you haven't done a damn thing since you got here except drink beer and try to sleep with the guests. This is the last straw, Luke." Bec turned to Penny. "You stay here, and I'll get the guys to bring a spare battery when they drop me off. Oh, and if you want to kick him in the balls a few times from me while you're here with him and no witnesses, be my guest."

Much though Penny wanted to beat the shit out of Luke, she didn't want to miss her date with Jay. "No, I'll walk," she said. "How far is it?"

"About fifteen, twenty minutes," Luke said. "Not far at all."

Penny nodded. She could manage that, even in a dress. She looked at Bec. "If the ball-kicking's still happening, would you do a bit for me?"

Bec grinned. "Gladly."

So Penny set off, figuring she had about an hour of

daylight left. She'd only need half of that, if Luke was right.

An hour later, still trudging along the track, Penny decided that Luke was wrong. She'd also decided that he was a dodgy bastard and she hoped Bec beat him to death by the time she got back. She was late for her date with Jay, starving for a dinner she should have eaten half an hour ago, and her mouth was too dry to swear at Luke, the universe and everything else. Still she kept going, as the moon gave her just enough light to see the track in front of her, but with no other lights in view, she wasn't sure how much farther she had to go until she reached the farm.

She lost track of time, concentrating just on putting one foot in front of the other, so when she rounded a clump of bushes and found herself on a lawn, an actual lawn, Penny dropped to her knees. Finally, she glimpsed lights up ahead, and heard the sound of running water, which turned out to be the artificial waterfall feeding the swimming pool.

The lights were the exit signs in the restaurant, which had closed for the night, by the look of it. The staff lived onsite, though, she was sure of it, so Penny stumbled through the compound until she found a house that the signs proclaimed was PRIVATE. That meant accommodation for staff, not tourists, she was certain.

She raised a weary arm to knock on the door. And again. And a third time, with some desperation. If no one answered, she was going to curl up on the veranda and cry herself to sleep. This was the worst night in the history of bad nights…

The door creaked open. "What is it?" a woman's voice croaked.

"I've come from the camp up on the ridge. The car

broke down and there's no battery for the radio." Tears leaked from Penny's eyes. "I was supposed to be here this afternoon, to see Jay. Is he…is he still here?"

The woman tugged her pyjama top down over her tummy. "Jay? You mean Jay Felix? He was here hours ago. Had a couple of drinks while he was waiting, but when you didn't turn up, he made Baz take him over to the camp by boat. Baz was back before it was dark, so he must have dropped him off and come straight back. Jay's not here."

Penny burst into tears. Fucking universe. It could go fuck itself with three cactuses. Three fucking huge, thorny cactuses, full of venomous tarantulas and…

"Oh, don't cry, love. Give me a sec. I'll find you a bed where you can sleep and Baz will run you back in the morning."

Penny only cried harder. "I'm supposed to spend tonight with Jay!" Not alone in some charity bed.

"Shush, love. Okay, I'll grab the keys and drive you back to camp, then. Too dangerous to take a boat out there with the tide out, and Baz is a bear if you wake him up, anyway."

Penny wiped her face with her dust-covered arm. "Thank you."

FIFTY-SIX

After twenty minutes' driving, Penny saw the dead four-wheel-drive looming out of the darkness in the newer vehicle's headlights. "Here," Penny said, glaring at the beer fridge she could now see beside the wheel, right where Bec said it would be. She wanted to kick it into pieces, but her feet hurt too much right now. In the morning, maybe.

She thanked the woman, whose name she couldn't remember, and slid out of the car. Her shoes hit sand with a crunch Penny hoped she never heard again. She was sick of sand.

Penny made her way to the darkened kitchen, grabbing a slice of stale bread to still her hunger. The fire pit was dark, too, and the whole place looked deserted. Luke's swag wasn't on the veranda where it usually lay. Penny hoped Bec had beaten him to death and buried him in an unmarked grave. Maybe in the cemetery, near all the other dead men, where no one would think to look.

She wanted to crawl into her tent and sleep for a week, but she needed to see Jay first. To tell him why she'd stood him up. So she dragged herself to his cabin and knocked on the door. When no one answered, she peeped inside to see if he was asleep. Both beds were empty, though a guitar case on the floor told her Jay hadn't vacated the place fully yet.

Penny gave up. She staggered up the hill to the bathroom, intending to freshen up before she fell into bed.

As she reached the steps, the sound of music reached her ears, borne by a surprisingly chilly night breeze. Penny shivered, folding her arms across her chest, as another gust of wind brought the sound of Jay's unmistakeable singing voice.

Unable to help herself, Penny faced into the breeze and followed the sound. The soft music seemed to give her a second wind, which she needed to climb the hill to the beehive tree, now ringed by dried roses that lay where they'd fallen when Melissa got stung. The melody lured her on, deeper into the dunes, where she knew the old pearl divers were buried. As she passed the second grave stone, she saw them, silhouetted against the sky on the crest of the ridge, where she and Calais had watched whales.

Jay sang again, a song she'd never heard before. After a moment, Calais joined in, her voice weaving around his in perfect harmony.

Penny stumbled and fell to her knees. Weary beyond belief, she listened to the haunting duet sung to ghosts in a graveyard, and she felt like a ghost, too. A fragment of the past, best forgotten, to make way for the future.

What was it Jay had said he wanted in that first video? Someone to inspire love songs so beautiful he could seduce the whole world, but there was only one woman in the world he wanted. *Is that woman you?* His invitation echoed in her mind.

No. No matter how much she wanted it to be, the answer was no. She loved him, as surely as the sun would rise in the morning, but the woman he wanted was Calais. The one who could sing in harmony with his heart.

Defeated, Penny dragged herself down the hill and into her lonely bed.

Go ahead and laugh, universe, she thought. She'd lost, but she hadn't lost as much as Calais. It was time to let the other girl win, and wish her the best.

FIFTY-SEVEN

Penny slept badly. Every time she closed her eyes, it felt like she was walking through sand in endless darkness, never reaching her destination. She'd jolt awake to make sure she wasn't sleepwalking, then doze off and dream about walking again.

What finally brought her out of dreamland was the smell of bacon. Not the aroma of someone slowly warming it until the fat melted in the pan, then letting it sizzle until it was just crisp without drying out. No, this was bacon burning, at the hand of an idiot who had the grill turned up too high.

Luke. It had to be.

Penny shucked off her sleeping bag, ripped open the tent zip and marched to the kitchen, her hands itching to shove Luke's face against the hot grill until he was scarred for life.

But when she reached the veranda, she saw that it wasn't Luke. It wasn't Bec, either.

Jay stood at the barbeque, tongs in hand, batting at the hissing, spitting bacon when it tried to jump off the grill.

"Turn that down," Penny said, reaching for the burner knobs. "You're murdering good bacon."

"I'm sorry," he said, sounding subdued.

Penny sighed. "Don't be. I'm sure most rock stars have personal chefs who cook their bacon for them. Most people get it wrong, anyway. You're supposed to – "

"No, I'm sorry," Jay repeated. "About last night."

Penny closed her eyes, not wanting him to see how much she still hurt. "Me, too."

"I was looking forward to our date last night," he continued. "I wanted a chance to talk to you alone. To get to know you better when you're not cooking. Mostly because I feel like such an idiot, when you're schooling me on how to cook on a bloody barbeque. I'm an Aussie bloke. This sort of thing should be in my blood, but all I can do is burn stuff."

Penny cracked a smile. "That's what most Aussie blokes do, all right."

"I'm sorry. I didn't know the whole story until Baz dropped by this morning. He was supposed to pick us all up, but I figured I'd let you sleep a little longer, and so I stayed, too. I want to try and make up for what happened last night. I wanted to make you breakfast, a sort of a date, but…" He swore as some of the bacon started smoking.

Penny grabbed another set of tongs from the kitchen and did her best to save his bacon. "So there's just the two of us, but bacon for…well, a small army. Any eggs?"

Jay shook his head. "I waited at the restaurant last night. When we couldn't raise the camp on the radio, I made Baz bring me out here. Luke told me about the car breaking down and the radio going dead, and how you'd gone for a walk. He said you'd be back soon."

"He's a dickhead and a liar," Penny snarled. "He said it was fifteen minutes' walk to the pearl farm. It took me hours!"

"That's what Baz said. He took Bec back to the farm because she wanted to call her office, and Luke went with her. That left you, me and Calais, and when I told her I wanted to spend the last morning alone with you, she said she understood and headed over to the resort alone. I'm sorry."

"It's all right." It wasn't, but Penny felt she should say it. He sounded so sad, and none of it was his fault. It was that bastard, Luke, conniving with the universe. "When I made it back last night, I heard you two. You sound...so good together." That, at least, was true.

Jay grinned. "You think so?"

Penny nodded, not trusting her voice, as her eyes filled with tears. She wanted him, oh, so much, but Calais...

Warm arms enfolded her, hugging her to his chest. Fingers stroked her hair, soothing, as she cried for everything that could have been, if the world weren't so fucked up.

"Penelope, look at me."

Reluctantly, she lifted her head, not wanting to look into those warm, brown eyes with her own red-rimmed ones.

"I'm so sorry."

The way he looked at her, like he was begging to kiss

her. Without thinking, she stretched up to grant his desire. And hers. God, yes. And hers.

At only a breath away, she regained her senses. Calais. Those lips were Calais' to kiss, not hers.

With her heart in her throat, Penny forced herself to pull away. "I have to pack." She hurried back to her tent and started to throw her things back into her bag. If this had all happened last night, it would be fine, but he'd chosen Calais and she respected that. She should be fucking happy for her, that Calais got an incredible man like Jay.

She repeated it so many times to herself over the course of the day that it had become a mantra by the time she stood in the resort's pub with Calais and the camera crew, waiting for Jay to officially announce his decision. A mantra to keep herself from crying. Because no one deserved to see her cry. Especially not the happy couple.

FIFTY-EIGHT

Jason stopped on the veranda outside the Jungle, forcing himself to breathe deeply. He almost laughed at himself, getting jittery about walking into a pub. That had to be a first for him.

One more breath. In through his nostrils, before whistling out through his teeth, bared in a cocky grin he definitely didn't feel right now. Jason patted his pocket to make sure the box was still there, ready for the lucky girl he intended to propose to in a few minutes.

Rock stars don't get nervous, he told himself. We just get on with the fucking show and knock 'em all dead.

He strode through the palm trees, past the cameras to Paige's side.

Paige burbled some sort of introduction, but Jason didn't hear it. His attention was transfixed on the two girls standing opposite him. Both Calais and Penelope looked like they were going to a ball. Formal dresses, hair styled in rigid curls and swirls, and as much makeup as Paige. Brides, that's what they looked like, he realised as his heart sank. Or bridesmaids.

He'd promised them a show, and Paige had certainly met him halfway. Whoever he chose would be ready for the photo shoot he was certain Paige had planned for afterwards. After he'd proposed to one of them, and hopefully she'd accepted.

Fuck. Why was this so hard?

Phuong, that's why. And Audra. He'd proposed to both of them, and both had ripped out his heart and stomped on it.

But that wasn't going to happen tonight. He wouldn't let it.

Paige's voice cut through his reverie. "Jay?"

"Yeah?"

Paige hitched her smile up a notch so she beamed at him. "Which of these lovely ladies do you choose?"

Jason shook his head slowly, wanting to spin this out properly. He'd promised drama and suspense and all that shit. This was his show. "First, I got a couple of gifts for the girls. To remember me by, as if they'd ever forget." He winked at the camera.

Paige forced out a laugh, but the panic in her eyes told Jason she didn't like losing control one little bit. Tough.

Jason nodded to Marcel, the barman, who pulled a beribboned tube from behind the bar and threw it. His aim was slightly off, but Jason easily moved to intercept the parcel's flight, plucking it out of mid-air as he had so many times onstage.

No screams or cheering accompanied this performance. He kind of missed it. His grin didn't fade as he crossed the floor to stand before Penelope and bowed, holding the gift in his outstretched hands. "A present for you."

"Oh." Penelope's hands shook as she took the gift. She tore through the paper, then held her prize aloft. "A microphone. Oh my God, it looks like the same one from…"

"Our karaoke night," Jason finished for her. "Sure is. And I signed it for you, too." He backed away from her to accept the second gift from Marcel. This one was too big to throw, dwarfing the bow someone had tied to the carry handle. There was no disguising this gift.

Jason's eyes met Calais' as he strode past Penelope to present the other girl with her parting gift.

Calais swallowed, her eyes glittering with what looked like tears. Oh fuck, crying women – the last thing he needed. Jason thrust the box at her, hoping it would distract her enough to stop her from crying.

Calais grasped the handle with both hands, and for a moment Jason thought it was too heavy for her as she lowered it to the floor. Then she dropped to her knees on the tiles, heedless of her dress, as she opened the case to see what was inside. She gasped, her hands hovering over the guitar.

"I signed that, too," he said, pointing.

Calais barely glanced at the autograph. She looked like she was itching to pull the Gibson into her arms and play, just like she had that night in the dunes, but she appeared to change her mind and closed the case again without touching the guitar at all. She rose to her feet, hugging the case to her chest. "Thank you."

"If you ever want another jam session with me, bring that, and you're on," he said, his eyes searching hers. Would she want it, or would the guitar be on an online auction site by morning?

"Thank you," Calais repeated. "I will. When…when I'm ready." Not yet, in other words.

Jason's shoulders slumped, though not as much as Calais'. He knew how much healing time could do. But sometimes it took a shitload of time.

Paige clapped her hands, trying to draw attention back to her. "How sweet! You bought them both presents. But you can't have both ladies, Jay, though we know your reputation. There can only be one winner here tonight. So tell me, Jay. Has the rock star decided which girl he wants to be his wife?"

Everyone who'd been at the dinner had said the same thing when Paige interviewed them: they wanted him to pick Calais. Quiet, unassuming, mourning Calais. The press would rip her apart and the trolls would fight over what remained. He'd have to protect her, or things would be worse than they'd ever been with Paige.

Then there was Penelope, who the staff hadn't mentioned at all. Who'd walked miles to the pearl farm just to go on a date with him. A fighter to the core, certainly. Down to earth, but she dressed up nice. She made pancakes that could have come from heaven. If a reporter said something she didn't like, she'd probably punch him. Or her.

No. Yes. No. Jason eased the box out of his pocket, opening it and holding it up to the light so the cameras could get a good look at the huge pink-purple diamond. He thought it was hideous, but it had been donated by the local diamond mine, and he hadn't been able to refuse it.

Collective gasps from all three women – and some of the camera crew – told him they didn't mind men bearing huge pink-purple things that formed big bulges in their pants pockets.

Jason took one final, deep breath. Time to decide.

FIFTY-NINE

Penny couldn't cool the heat in her cheeks. She didn't normally blush, so why was she doing it now? It was Jay. The raw sexuality of the man, and remembering the way he'd held her through their duet in this very bar. Never mind that she'd sung like one of the screeching lorikeets in the trees outside, or that she'd forgotten half the words. It had been like there was no one else in the world but the two of them that night. How could any man compare to him?

Her fingers tightened around the microphone. She'd keep it forever, as a souvenir of their time together. No matter how shitty life got, she'd remember that for a short time, it had been wonderful once. And it would be again.

He gave Calais a guitar. Penny suppressed a snort. At least her gift would fit in her suitcase. Where would she put a guitar? Calais could barely lift the case. And it's not like

Jay even played the guitar. He was the band's lead singer. Everyone knew that. A microphone was way more personal than something huge like a guitar. It probably wasn't even a good one – just something cheap one of the production assistants had picked up for him in town. It's not like there was a music shop in town.

Paige waved her hands to get Penny's attention, gesturing for the girls to stand up straight again. Lined up for a firing squad, as Jay picked one and the cameras zoomed in on the other.

I won't cry, Penny swore. She might have given the cameras a blush, but she wouldn't give them a single tear to gloat over. She'd gotten what she wanted, the chance to be on TV and save her reputation. She'd signed the contract for the cooking show. Calais could have the delicious rock star, Penny thought, as her eyes bade farewell to the well-muscled calves, vanishing into low-slung shorts that exposed the delectable, muscular V pointing to the ever-present bulge in the front of his pants. Sure, he wore a shirt, but he hadn't buttoned it, so the cameras could zoom in on that toned, tanned six-pack that gleamed like it had been oiled. Maybe it had. After all, the makeup crew had slathered their stuff on her and Calais. They'd probably attacked Jay with foundation, lip gloss and anything else they could think of, just for a chance to get their hands on him.

Those girls got paid to oil him up, she realised, wishing she'd chosen a different career path. Maybe she could…

Paige clapped her hands. "So tell me, Jay. Has the rock star decided which girl he wants to be his wife?"

Wife? No, that never happened on these shows. Not

someone he'd only known for a few short weeks. Not even rock stars fell in love that fast. She was just saying lines, something to get people at home excited when they watched the show. It didn't mean anything. It couldn't.

Jay pulled something out of his pocket, showing that not all that bulging had been…Jay.

Oh God, she wasn't blushing again, was she? Just the thought of Jay naked…

The diamond caught the light and all thought ceased. Rock. Ring. Huge. Fuck…

Something bumped into Penny's side and grasped her hand. Calais. The girl looked terrified, Penny thought. Like she wasn't ready to wear a rock that big. But who was, really?

This time, Penny didn't hesitate. She squeezed Calais' hand with all the support she could muster and managed a reassuring smile. While Penny would give almost anything for Jay to choose her, Calais deserved happiness with him more. God knew she'd had precious little lately, and Penny had more than her fair share. A show. A spot on a cooking show.

As long as she didn't give the cameras or the bitchy host the satisfaction of seeing her cry.

Jay dropped to his knees, holding the ring up like the offering it was.

Penny squeezed her eyes shut, breathing steadily in the desperate hope to stem the tears. Tears of happiness for the friend beside her, she told herself, though the TV crew wouldn't see it that way. Calais' clammy fingers tightened around hers.

Penny heard Jay clear his throat. "Will you marry me?"

SIXTY

Xan had spent the whole day vacillating between wanting to go to the pub to watch Jay propose to his bride, and wanting to stay the hell away from the media circus she knew it would be. So staged, artificial and unrealistic…could he actually love one of the girls he'd just met?

She snorted. If it was her, she'd take one look at the hideous pink rock, then at the man she barely knew, and tell him how ridiculous a marriage proposal was, under the circumstances. If a man wanted her love, he had to earn it. Not four weeks of romance, in between seducing multiple other girls, before declaring his undying love for a stranger.

Surely even Jay Felix wasn't that stupid.

Xan laughed. She'd seen Jay do some damn stupid things in the year she'd known him. Swimming naked in the lagoon every morning, marrying a mail-order bride bigamist, driving while drunk and losing his licence, buying a girl's virginity at auction, jumping out of a helicopter, playing golf on the roof...and now this.

No, proposing marriage to a stranger wasn't out of the ordinary for Jay Felix. He had crazy for breakfast every morning. Right before his nude morning swim.

And his way with women...no matter who they were, he made them feel like they mattered. Phuong, Flavia, even Gaia...he'd made them feel like the only woman in the world, the only one who mattered to him. He made them fall head over heels in love with him, on top of that perfect body of his.

If he wasn't the bane of her existence, would she have fallen for his charms, too? Xan mused. No. Definitely not. She'd continue to enjoy watching his morning performance in the water, of course, but that didn't mean she liked him. Couldn't stand him, in fact. But the woman who did hold his heart would be a lucky one indeed, if only because he'd do everything to make her believe his world revolved around her. How could any woman resist that sort of adoration?

Maybe she'd be wrong. Maybe one of them would have the sense to tell him how ridiculous the whole set up was, or tell him an outright no. Anything was better than a nauseating yes, followed by kisses and hyperventilation. Which girl had Jay decided on, anyway?

Curiosity pulled Xan out of her office and halfway across the foyer before she heard the receptionist calling her name.

Xan halted. "What, Philly?"

"Phone call for you, Ms Lane. A Mr Rome from

Broome Backpackers. He says it's urgent."

What could the backpackers have to ask her now? She hadn't worked there for a year. It's not like any of the guests there could afford to stay at Romance Island Resort. Or take one of the day trips.

"What does he want?"

Philly shrugged. "He won't say. Just that it's urgent and he has to speak to you."

Xan sighed. "Put him through to my office phone. I'll take the call in there." She marched back into her office, flicking the lights on. She didn't much care who Jay chose, anyway. At least it wouldn't be the one who'd embezzled her company's money to pay for plastic surgery. Those unnatural boobs that didn't bounce one bit…

Xan lifted the receiver to her ear. "This is Xan Lane, the hotel manager at Romance Island Resort. How can I help you?"

The man on the other end burst into hysterical laughter. "Oh, thank God! I thought I'd lost you. Baby, it's me. I've come halfway round the world to tell you I was wrong. You're the only one that I want. You and no one else."

"Who is this?" Xan demanded, her heart sinking as suspicion built in the back of her mind.

"It's Jerome, baby, your fiancé. I'm in Broome, at the backpackers where you used to work. They gave me the number of your new place when I explained who I was. I'm here to marry you and take you back home where you belong, baby."

The phone slipped from Xan's nerveless hand and smashed on the floor.

SIXTY-ONE

"Will you marry me?" Jay repeated, a note of urgency in his voice.

Penny opened her eyes to look at Calais, only to find the girl's shining eyes firmly fixed on her.

What on Earth…?

Penny dropped her gaze to the rock star kneeling before her, holding up that blindingly beautiful diamond, but it was his eyes that mesmerised her. Warm, caramel brown that she could drown in as he stared up at her.

Her knees grew weak and tears sprang to her eyes. She wouldn't cry. She wouldn't. She…

"Will you, Penelope?" Jay's hot caramel sauce voice implored, melting her heart into mush.

"Oh my God, yes!"

The story continues in
The Rock Star's Wedding

ABOUT THE AUTHOR

Demelza Carlton has always loved the ocean, but on her first snorkelling trip she found she was afraid of fish.

She has since swum with sea lions, sharks and sea cucumbers and stood on spray drenched cliffs over a seething sea as a seven-metre cyclonic swell surged in, shattering a shipwreck below.

Demelza now lives in Perth, Western Australia, the shark attack capital of the world.

The *Ocean's Gift* series was her first foray into fiction, followed by her suspense thriller *Nightmares* trilogy. She swears the *Mel Goes to Hell* series ambushed her on a crowded train and wouldn't leave her alone.

Want to know more? You can follow Demelza on Facebook, Twitter, YouTube or her website, Demelza Carlton's Place at:

www.demelzacarlton.com

Books by Demelza Carlton

Ocean's Gift series

Ocean's Gift (#1)
Ocean's Infiltrator (#2)
Ocean's Depths (#3)
Water and Fire

Turbulence and Triumph series

Ocean's Justice (#1)
Ocean's Trial (#2)
Ocean's Triumph (#3)
Ocean's Ride (#4)
Ocean's Cage (#5)
Ocean's Birth (#6)
How To Catch Crabs

Nightmares Trilogy

Nightmares of Caitlin Lockyer (#1)
Necessary Evil of Nathan Miller (#2)
Afterlife of Alana Miller (#3)

Mel Goes to Hell series

Welcome to Hell (#1)
See You in Hell (#2)
Mel Goes to Hell (#3)
To Hell and Back (#4)
The Holiday From Hell (#5)
All Hell Breaks Loose (#6)

Romance Island Resort series

Maid for the Rock Star (#1)
The Rock Star's Email Order Bride (#2)
The Rock Star's Virginity (#3)
The Rock Star and the Billionaire (#4)
The Rock Star Wants A Wife (#5)
The Rock Star's Wedding (#6)